W9-BCF-030

THE MAN FROM
INTERNAL
AFFAIRS

BOOKS BY NAT HENTOFF

MUSIC

HEAR ME TALKING TO YA (with Nat Shapiro)
JAZZ (with Albert McCarthy)
JAZZ IS
THE JAZZ LIFE
THE JAZZ MAKERS (with Nat Shapiro)
JOURNEY INTO JAZZ (for very young readers)

NONFICTION

THE NEW EQUALITY
OUR CHILDREN ARE DYING
PEACE AGITATOR: THE STORY OF A. J. MUSTE
A POLITICAL LIFE: THE EDUCATION OF JOHN V. LINDSAY
STATE SECRETS: POLICE SURVEILLANCE IN AMERICA
(with Paul Cowan and Nick Egleson)
THE FIRST FREEDOM: THE TUMULTUOUS HISTORY OF
FREE SPEECH IN AMERICA

NOVELS FOR ADULTS

CALL THE KEEPER
ONWARDS!
BLUES FOR CHARLIE DARWIN

NOVELS FOR YOUNG READERS

I'M REALLY DRAGGED BUT NOTHING GETS ME DOWN
IN THE COUNTRY OF OURSELVES
JAZZ COUNTRY
THIS SCHOOL IS DRIVING ME CRAZY
DOES THIS SCHOOL HAVE CAPITAL PUNISHMENT?
THE DAY THEY CAME TO ARREST THE BOOK

NAT HENTOFF

THE MAN FROM
INTERNAL
AFFAIRS

THE MYSTERIOUS PRESS • New York

The Mysterious Press, 129 West 56th Street, New York, N.Y. 10019

Printed in the United States of America
First Printing: October 1985
10 9 8 7 6 5 4 3 2 1

Library of Congress Cataloging-in-Publication Data

Hentoff, Nat.
    The man from Internal Affairs.

    I. Title.
PS3558.E575M3   1985   813'.54   85-15248
ISBN 0-89296-141-4

THE MAN FROM
INTERNAL AFFAIRS

1

The detective's voice was low and flat. "You have a right to remain silent. So long as you can stand the pain."

On the edge of the chair in front of him a short, blunt-bodied man with the head of an indignant turtle looked up at the tall bony detective and said in a fat, gurgling voice, "I bet you only use that asshole humor on your brothers, ain't that right, Mr. Detective McKibbon, sir?"

Sam McKibbon looked out the window at the kids playing in the spring sunlight on East Fifth Street. He didn't know any of them by name. For the time being. Looking at the suspect again, McKibbon said, "Well, you going to call a lawyer or do you want us to scare you up one?"

"I'm going to testify to what you said—'so long as you can stand the pain.' "

"Tell me about it," McKibbon looked at his watch. "Tell you what, why don't you confess, then you can say I coerced you. You're a gambling man. Might be worth a shot."

The turtle stuck out a black tongue. "That was no rape. I been banging that bitch for years."

McKibbon yawned. Be nice to fall asleep on the grass in the park. But shit, you'd get a needle up your ass. "All right-ee," the detective looked at the hard-shelled black man, thinking how satisfying it would be to step on him and feel that crunch, "It's your play." He pointed to the phone.

The suspect began to dial. Coming across the squadroom straight toward McKibbon was Captain Fortunato Randazzo, commander of the Ninth Precinct, a position to which he had been promoted six months before. He had since been heard to mutter that forces unknown in the hierarchy at One Police Plaza were conspiring to kill him. "They sent me to this fucking overflowing garbage can because they knew it'd give me a stroke. The perfect crime, those bastards."

Poking his finger into McKibbon's chest, Randazzo, a big man with black curly hair he couldn't believe was still black, roared, "Where the hell's Noah? His vacation was up two hours ago. What does he think, he's been around the block so many times he doesn't have to go by the rules anymore?"

McKibbon glanced at the turtle whispering into the phone. "My fault, Captain. Noah called me at home last night. Shannon wasn't feeling so good so he figured they wouldn't get back on the road as early as he'd thought. She's almost ready to pop, you know. Got to be careful. I told him they shouldn't have made the trip."

"Nothing's going to be wrong with her," Randazzo said. "Young and strong as she is. He's the one who should worry about being pregnant at his age. Anyway, thanks for giving me the message. Any others you got in your pocket, like from last month, last year? You know, if it's too hard for you to remember, you could make a mark in ink on your hand."

"You got any white ink, Captain?"

"Sensitive, sensitive. Chees, everybody around here has such tender feelings it's a wonder you're not all puking all the time. I want to see Green soon's he comes in. You think you can remember that without dropping everything else?"

McKibbon smiled. "You know how it is, Cap'n. What was that you said?"

"It's a plot," Randazzo said, walking away. "They want to kill me. And they got McKibbon in on it. Whenever a dago gets too high, that's what happens. Remember Cassius," he turned back to McKibbon, "as soon as he comes in, I want to know. I got a new partner for him while you're gone."

2

The next morning, on the twelfth floor of police head-quarters at One Police Plaza in downtown Manhattan, Chief Wilfred Mulvaney, head of the Internal Affairs Division of the police department, was at his desk. The IAD is charged with policing the police—uncovering corruption and all other form of criminal behavior, conceivable and inconceivable, in the department.

The Chief's office was at the back, past a reception area and past rows of file cabinets whose contents were secured by padlocks and steel bars.

Wilfred Mulvaney was a tall, ample man in his late fifties, with thick, wavy silver hair, horn-rimmed bifocals, and a habitual air of pleasurable anticipation. If his window shades were not always down, he could have seen part of Chinatown from his office windows. Instead, he was able to see, on his walls, a large numbered map of the police precincts in the five boroughs; a color photograph of a suspicious polar bear and her two frolicking cubs; autographed photographs of John F. Kennedy, James Michael Curley, and Adam Clayton Powell; and a print of Sir Thomas More. On the wall directly opposite the Chief's desk was a sheet of white paper framed in wood and bearing the reminder:

NIMIS PROBAT, NIHIL PROBAT

On the Chief's desk, in addition to large, neat stacks of

papers, was a photograph of three tall, dark-haired, young men in their twenties stiffly arranged behind a seated, slender, stern, brown-haired woman in her late forties. Next to the photograph is a vase, containing, this May morning, a yellow rose.

Also on the Chief's desk was the morning mail. Nobody else was allowed to open the Chief's mail because the sources of information in the Internal Affairs Division are very closely held; it was Chief Mulvaney who decided— when the sources appeared in the mail—who held them. Sometimes only he did.

This morning, one of the letters had no return name or address. Mulvaney took it up by a corner and set it aside, but close to him. When he had sorted the rest of the mail, Mulvaney, a fingernail on the bottom edge of the letter without a return address, slowly slit it open with a small knife in his other hand.

On a single sheet of lined yellow paper, someone—there was no signature—had printed:

THIS IS TO INFORM YOU OF CORRUPTION IN THE NINTH PRECINCT.
A DETECTIVE IS SELLING INFORMATION TO ONE OR MORE DEFENSE ATTORNEYS. HIS NAME IS NOAH GREEN. HIS PARTNER, SAMUEL McKIBBON, APPEARS TO BE CLEAN. YOU ALSO OUGHT TO LOOK INTO THE HANDLING OF EVIDENCE BY THE MAJOR CASE SQUAD.

Mulvaney scratched his nose, whistled a few bars of "The Wild Colonial Boy," and picked up the phone. "Jeremy," he said softly.

A thin, bald, slightly stooped man, about forty, with a pasty face and bright black eyes, came in, looked to the desk, bent over, his hands in his pockets, and read the yellow legal sheet.

"He doesn't give a fuck about the Major Case Squad," Jeremy said. "He stuck that in so it doesn't look like a vendetta against this Green."

"Who is he—our helpful friend?" the Chief looked at the letter and then at Jeremy.

"Got to be a cop. Who the hell ever heard of the Major Case Squad on the outside?"

"Maybe," the Chief said. "Could be a buff though. But a buff would pick something more, uh, vivid. Like homicide. I'll go along with you, Jeremy. Provisionally. Now, as to the allegation. As I recall, the only associate we have in the Ninth is just a couple of months out of the Academy. If there's anything to this, he's got no way to get into it, not a green kid in uniform. And if he tried to find a way, they'd be on to him and chew him right up, poor boy."

"Randall Dickerson's down there now," Jeremy said. "After you got him promoted to detective when he finished with us, he went to Midtown South, and now he's at the Ninth."

Mulvaney took out a box of Dunhills and lit one. "It's been a long time since he worked for us. A very long time. He came right out of the Academy too, but he was a whiz from the start. A wonder at covering his ass. Still, he probably doesn't like us anymore, filled as he is by now with the milk of loyalty to his buddies, both the good guys and the sleazebags. However, Jeremy, why don't you find out, very quiet, how Randall fits in down there, especially how he fits with Green? Then maybe we'll talk with Randall. I don't think he'd want to turn down a request from his former rabbi."

The Chief looked again at the sheet of yellow paper. "And see what you can find on this Green fellow. Without asking, you understand."

"Fortunato Randazzo is the new commander of the Ninth," Jeremy said, looking speculatively at Mulvaney.

"Oh, no, he's the last person I want in on this. He'd take

it so personally, one of his men under suspicion, he'd blow the whole thing up, trying to nail Green before we do. No, we'll do it our usual way. Just by ourselves. Sweet and slow. Ever hear that Fats Waller record, 'Sweet and Slow'?"

Jeremy said he had not, and later kicked himself for not lying.

3

Two weeks later, a little before seven in the morning, a thin, wiry Puerto Rican in his late teens, with the look of a generous pirate, was walking along Avenue C on the Lower East Side. He was whistling a fiercely graceful melodic line while accompanying himself with staccato raps on the tops of cars, the shutters of stores, and his own head. With admiration, he stopped to look at his lean, hard hands, ached to apply them to a real conga drum but was about to settle for the cover of a garbage can when he saw a hand coming out of that can.

He took a handkerchief out of his back pocket and very slowly lifted the lid. Very quickly he put it back and ran, searching his pockets for a quarter, to a pay phone on the corner.

"Shit," he said, when he saw that the phone had been yanked out of the booth and that the booth itself was none too steady. "Shit," he banged his fist on his knee, "where the hell do I think I am?"

Sprinting up the next block, he came to a bodega, looked in the window, saw a youngster his own age unloading a case of milk, and knocked hard on the pane.

"Got a phone?" he asked as the door was opened.

The other boy pointed toward the back of the store, picked his nose judiciously, and went out into the street where he took pleasure in barking at a cat.

At the phone in the back of the bodega, the teenager

dialed a number, heard a deep grunt, and said, "Rise and shine, early bird gets the worm and have I got a big one for you today. Garbage can, on Avenue C, east side of C, near the corner of Second, in front of that TV repair place."

"What's *in* the fucking can?" a raw voice asked at the other end. It was followed by a woman's voice: "Noah, Noah, anything wrong?" And that was followed by the wail of a baby.

"Somebody that once was but is no more," said the teenager. "The body's in the garbage, but the soul is shining somewhere. Hey, how about that? You could put it to music. I can hear Stevie Wonder with a bass clarinet, a trumpet with a tight mute, strings—"

"Jesus, Angel, whattaya got?"

"A lady. I saw the head of a lady. I didn't want to disturb nothing, you understand?"

"Thanks," Noah Green said. "I owe you one."

"Yes, you do. The time will come."

"Have a nice day, pisher."

"Same to you, big putz."

4

Twenty minutes later, an unmarked car, with Randall Dickerson driving, picked up Noah Green. Dickerson, black, in his mid-thirties, looked ten years younger. Actually, Green was thinking as he moved his bulk into the other seat, the guy looks unmarked. Like Billy Eckstine. Smooth, real smooth, unmarked by anything.

"Where'd Sam go on his vacation?" Dickerson asked.

"Wyoming. Can you believe it? He's reading a travel magazine in a barbershop and all of a sudden, the one thing he wants to do more than anything in this life is go down the Snake River in a raft. He says he has to get clean, and that's the place."

"Think he'll be back?" Dickerson smiled straight ahead.

"I give him five days," Green said, "including travel time. Six, if he drowns in that goyishe river."

"I meant to ask you," Dickerson said, "that bronze plaque outside the precinct house. I just noticed it this morning. I mean, I've seen it before, but I never really saw it, you know. What's it about?"

"It says: 'Patrolman Rocco Laurie and Patrolman Gregory Foster. Slain while on patrol in the Ninth Precinct January 27, 1972.' It goes on to say, and I think I'm pretty close, 'They served their country in Vietnam as United States Marines and now give us in death a shining example of racial brotherhood that makes us proud to claim them as members of our band of brothers.'"

Dickerson was silent for a moment. "Did they *ask* to go out together?" he looked at Green.

"Not that I know of." Green smiled. "I think we're going to do just fine, Randall."

They passed a block with nothing in it but rubble and one gutted seven-story building with holes where the windows used to be. On one side of the building were proclamations in faded red paint:

NO HEAT, NO RENT.

"The whole trick," said Green, "is to let nature take its course. Now there's no heat, no rent, no tenants, no hassles."

Around the corner was a large sign in the top-floor window of a small office building. It said:

DR. FABBIO

And below the name was the drawing of a tooth. Nothing more.

"Once again," Green said, "you see natural adaptation, Kids come out of school and they don't know how to read, but when a tooth hurts, they have no trouble finding Dr. Fabbio."

Half a block down, a white man, in his early twenties, was getting out of a venerable green Volvo with New Jersey plates.

"We got no time for him," Green said. "When he gets to be a corpse, we'll stop for him."

As their car moved on, the young man from New Jersey, looking behind him more out of custom than concern, walked down the block and stopped before an abandoned building. A brick was missing, and in the space, the man from New Jersey slipped an envelope. After a few seconds, his envelope disappeared and another one came toward him. The young man put that envelope in his jacket pocket and, without looking around again, returned to his car and then to New Jersey.

5

At the same time as Green and Dickerson arrived at the garbage can, a tall, bone-thin man, all in beige, including his graceful cowboy hat and his skin, was leaning against the wall of an abandoned synagogue on East Seventh Street near Avenue D. There was no glass in the windows of the two-story building, which still, though barely, announced itself as Bais Hamedrash Hagadol Anshe Ungarin. The paneled door was rather imposing. It had no lock.

"Young man," the cowboy said in a soft, clear voice to Angel, who was bouncing by, "stay a moment."

"Like to, but I got to get to school, Arthur. See ya."

"Now." Arthur did not raise his voice.

With a sigh, Angel stopped, out of range of the long beige arms.

"You avoid me, young man," Arthur smiled very thinly.

"Come on, Arthur, you know I got to go to school and then I got to work where I can. You know what I got at home."

"That is a shame, what you have at home. Just sits there and drinks and sleeps all day and drinks and sleeps all night. I could do you a good turn, young man, but I suppose you're sentimental about your mother. Though I'm blessed if I know who would be hurt by her removal."

"Gonna hurt my campaign for governor, when it comes,

if it gets out I put out a contract on my mother." Angel manufactured a smile.

Arthur did not smile back. "I need an assistant," he said.

"An assistant for doing what?" Angel moved a half inch farther away.

"A hundred dollars a day, Sundays off. That's just for the probation period. Then it moves up dramatically."

"I got to know what I'm supposed to be doing." Angel flinched as he saw a long brown rat enter the synagogue through a hole in the paneled door.

"Quality control," Arthur slowly arched his back. "You shall be my eyes and ears on how certain things are going when I am occupied elsewhere."

"What kind of things?"

"Angel, you do not play dumb well."

"I'll be working for Chin or Rodriguez or who?"

"Go back to playing dumb. You'll be working for me. You want to be a wiseass, you'll wind up walking around without an ass."

"Why me? Why'd you pick me?"

"Because you're a retard and this is an equal opportunity industry. Why are you playing these games with me, Angel?"

Angel sat down and leaned against the fence of the abandoned synagogue. "I can't do it, Arthur."

Two more rats sauntered in the synagogue. Angel felt cold.

"Why?" Arthur's voice was even colder.

"Hey, how come you didn't do time, Arthur, when Noah Green busted you a couple of years ago?"

"Hah!" Arthur smiled. "I will allow you to distract me for a moment, because it is a useful story for a growing boy. Young man, one of the vilest lies they tell about us blacks and Latinos is that any Jew is smarter than the whole lot of us. Well, I tricked that Jew. He did bust me, but the first thing I asked him was where was his search warrant for him to go through me, and he starts talking about how he doesn't need one once he has made a valid arrest and while he goes on like this, the stupid Jew forgets to read me my rights."

"You mean, he admitted he didn't? In court."

"No, of course not. He's a cop. He lied. But he knew that I made him lie, and that ate at him and ate at him. A nigger made him fuck up so he had to lie. I gave him, you could say, a small cancer, and that was very satisfying."

"But how did you get off?" Angel asked.

"Oh, I never have my name on anything. That business, Barney's business, I was sort of the office manager and so I made sure there was nothing of me in its records."

"But the dealers and the whores they picked up, they knew you, they could have made themselves a deal by saying who you were."

Arthur caressed his turquoise belt buckle. "Young man, nobody in his right mind would identify me in a courtroom. Even someone insane would not do that. My goodness, I myself would hate to be anybody who would do that. Now, Angel, why are you not rushing to embrace this extraordinary career development opportunity I have offered you."

Angel stood up, braced himself, looked into Arthur's green eyes, and looked away. "The truth, okay. I want to go another way, Arthur. If I go with you now, I only got your way to go. You understand."

Arthur nodded. "You're too smart to go any other way but my way, young man. But I know, you must see for yourself. That's what youth is for. So go and see what is out there. And you will find out that the whole world is Avenue D, Angel. And Avenue A and B and C. It's all the same everywhere. Do it to them before they do it to you. From the beginning of time. And even before that. Have a nice day, young man."

6

At eight-fifteen that morning, on Eighth Avenue, in a coffee shop that had much of the charm of a subway rest room, Jeremiah Riordan sat waiting for the bar next door to open. In his late sixties, with abundant white hair and cold, light blue eyes, Riordan had once been the commander of the First Homicide Squad, and was now retired.

The New York Times was spread in front of him, but Riordan was looking out the window at the involuntarily early risers shuffling down into the subway.

"That one," Riordan said to the soft, round, red-haired woman of indeterminate age beside him, "the one with his eyes on the ground, last night or yesterday he did something that could get him thirty years without parole. It's not only that he won't look up; it's the way his whole body is waiting to be cuffed."

The red-haired woman took a tiny silver flask from her large tapestried pocketbook and poured a few drops of brandy into her coffee. "You could have it all wrong," she said in a hoarse, cheerful voice. "He could be an innocent man being *pursued* by a man with a contract.

Riordan shook his head and sighed. "I don't know why I bother. Why would a hit man waste time on an innocent man? You don't think things through, Claire."

"Yeah," she beamed at him, "Well, I could be as right as you about that bum." She patted Riordan's hand. "I know, I know. You miss the force, don't you, sweetie?"

"Do you miss waking up and knowing you've got your whole life ahead of you? Do you miss that, Claire? Do you miss being expected somewhere?"

She giggled. "And being *feared* somewhere. Ain't that what you mean, sweetie?"

Riordan allowed himself a pinched smile. "Oh, you don't need to be expected anywhere to be feared. Not at all." He looked at her, then looked at her again. "Well now, instead of next door, will you join me for an after-breakfast celebration of the life that is to come?"

She lowered her head and looked up at him through her bangs. "There is nothing I would rather do, Lieutenant. I have been dreaming of this moment since we first met."

"At twilight, only yesterday it was," he said softly, "when the big dago threw the yellow runt all the way down the top of the bar and knocked you over at the other end."

She smoothed back her hair. "And only you could see there was something new on the floor. Come, Jeremiah, I want to be in the dark and hear about murder."

7

The corpse had been severed at the waist. An exhaustive and quite disgusting search of hundreds of garbage cans, whole blocks devoted solely to garbage, cellars, dumpsters, and other places where pieces of a corpse might have been stashed had not produced the other half of the body of this white female in her early twenties. The top half was being explored by the medical examiner.

"This one that schmuck will do himself," Green said as he and Dickerson settled into a booth at a coffee shop on Second Avenue. "It'll be in the papers, on the wire services, on television, and right in the middle of it, his teeny moustache twitching, will be Dr. Harvey Bloustein. You want to bet that before it's over he'll have misplaced the top part of her? They actually lost one of my corpses down there. Fortunately, the defendant had killed two people."

A waitress materialized and took their order. "Randazzo is going to be very, very upset." Green lit a cigar. "Drives him crazy when parts are missing. We still got a case, three years old, no head, no legs. Found in the river. Nude. Sometimes I walk into his office and Randazzo is staring at that file, growling. I mean growling."

"She was pretty, underneath all that garbage," Dickerson said.

"Not my type." Green speared a sausage. "Too young, too underdeveloped." He took a swig of Diet 7-Up. "Still. Anyway, I don't think she was just dumped here. She was here for something, probably dope. Crime-scene guys got some pictures of her. Her face wasn't marked too bad. We'll get a batch and show them around."

"You haven't heard from any of your snitches?" Dickerson asked.

"Not yet. Some of them don't come out of their coffins until evening."

"And the anonymous call that woke you up, the voice still doesn't ring any bells?"

"Nope," Green lied.

8

At one that afternoon, one of New York City's preeminent lawyers, according to a front-page profile that day in the *National Law Journal*, left his office on lower Broadway for lunch. In his early fifties, Jason Mendelssohn looked like the little train that could and that never stopped proving it. The short, muscular advocate barreled through crowds, crossed against the lights, either reading a brief or talking into a tape recorder, or both.

Mendelssohn had never been seen in repose. Not even in sleep, for he slept in a room separate from that of his wife. Not because of any hostility between them but because he liked having voluminous papers of his current cases next to him so that if an idea struck him in the middle of the night, he could get to work on it while still in bed.

His gray-black hair was short and bristly. And he had only one arm. Mendelssohn refused to disclose where his left arm had gone, or if he'd ever had one, and he refused to be fitted with an artificial limb; "I'd be worrying all the time the damn thing would fall off in front of the jury," he'd say, "and in this town the fucking jury would figure it was a pitch for sympathy and kick the hell out of my client."

Mendelssohn and Noah Green had gone to Boys' High in Brooklyn together, and both had been deliriously obsessed with jazz. While their classmates could recite the earned run averages of the entire pitching staff of the Brooklyn Dodgers, the New York Giants, and the Yankees, Mendels-

20

sohn and Green continually tested each other's knowledge of recording personnel and changes in big bands and combos.

Like: What now famous avant-garde pianist worked with Johnny Hodges's small combo after the Rabbit (Hodges) left the Duke (Ellington)?

"Cecil Taylor!" Mendelssohn would roar with all his might.

Every six months or so, Mendelssohn and Green would have lunch. Unless Green were testifying against, or had been involved in the apprehension of, a Mendelssohn client. Then the lunch would wait until the trial was over.

"Nu, so what else is new?" Mendelssohn said as he took a gulp of beer at Gudaitis's Bar and Grill on Essex Street where nobody fashionable, including the better class of criminals, ate. "I already knew as much as you told me about Blondie. She's all over *The Post*. At least half of her is."

Neither Green nor Mendelssohn liked spending much money in restaurants, and so Gudaitis's was a favorite of theirs. They had kept to their boyhood convictions: "When you spend money on food, what have you got left? But if you buy a book or a record. . . ."

"Listen," Mendelssohn eyed his pastrami on rye with as much anticipation as if he were cross-examining it, "I want to ask you something."

Green bit into a half-sour pickle. "So ask."

"It's about my boy."

"Yeah, he should have his degree by now."

"With honors," Mendelssohn scowled. "With honors in philosophy. Okay, so he'll never have enough money to let *his* kid get honors in philosophy unless I give it to him. But I could live with him being a professor somewhere. It's got some class. But my son the *shmendrick* doesn't want to teach philosophy. Doesn't want to teach, even if I bought him an endowed chair. He wants to be," Mendelssohn took another swig of beer, "actively involved with the times in which he lives."

"Like his daddy."

"No, no," Mendelssohn snarled. "Lawyers are too tricky, he says, too manipulative, too full of themselves. Thank you very much, you creep. You thought the money was dirty, why didn't you leave home? Anyway, Abner has found his true calling. Last summer, he worked—for nothing, of course—on *The Fire Island News*, and he had a byline, he had several bylines. Never in his whole life did he feel so good, even when he used to have a feedbag full of pot in front of his face all day. What I'm asking, and I'm embarrassed already—when's the last time you saw me embarrassed?"

"When you called Miss Neapolitano, our fifth-grade teacher, a *mamser* and you didn't know she was Jewish, just married to an Italian."

"Yeah, but she was a *mamser*. Boy, was she a *mamser*! So, you think Shannon can do anything for my son the yo-yo?"

"The best way to deal with Shannon is direct. Call her. She'll be going back to the paper as soon as she finds somebody she trusts to take care of the baby during the day, but she knows what's going on down there, if there are any openings, and for what."

Mendelssohn signaled for more beer. "Keep this to yourself, huh? I don't want it to get around that I ask favors from cops. Then I'll be swamped with clients, I'll never get home, and one day I'll keel over in my office for good. You got to think ahead, Noah."

9

The next morning at seven, an old black man, thin but not frail, his back ruler-straight, his eyes straight ahead, walked three times around the block and then stopped at the newsstand at St. Mark's Place. He picked up a *Times*, a *Wall Street Journal*, and three packs of Lucky Strikes.

"You know," the fat newsdealer said to Angel, "they could drop the fucking bomb right there," he pointed to the sidewalk in front of his stand, "and the next morning, people burned to a crisp all over the street, other people puking with poison, and that guy will be coming up here, taking his morning walk around the block, and stopping for his papers. Every damn morning he comes, same time to the second. Never said hello once. Never said nothing. I could be a machine you put a quarter in. I don't know who he is, I don't know what he does. I mean, fourteen years this has been going on. It's creepy."

"I know what he does, Sol," Angel said airily. "Well, I know what he did. He was one of them court stenographers. Guess he got too old. Now he's a messenger."

"How the hell'd you find that out?"

"I was curious, like you, so I gave myself an assignment. I do that a lot. I send myself a lot of places. Anyway, I follow the old guy to work. I take a quick look and see if one of my people works in the office, and one does, and I find out what I want to know. Nothing to it."

The newsstand owner shook his head. "You never cease to

amaze me, Angel. You're so fucking smart, so why don't you know that if you stay around here, you got to be dead by Christmas. If not this year, next year."

Angel grinned. "Where am I supposed to go, Sol? You gonna take me home to Jersey with you?"

"Ahh, I was just kidding. You'll finish high school, you'll go to college, you'll come back here running for mayor, and you wouldn't even know my name anymore."

"I'll tell you one thing." Angel was not smiling. "I worry about that old guy. He never says nothing to anybody and sooner or later, somebody's going to take that personal. It's like the old guy is asking for it. 'You won't notice me? I'm not good enough to be noticed?' Pow! It'll be somebody new in the neighborhood, not somebody who's used to him."

"Angel, you're always thinking. My son should have that disease. You know, Jews are not what they used to be. Where the smarts are coming from now, I see it down here every day, are from the Orientals, West Indians, and people like you, you know. I think maybe we Jews have had our time."

"That's an interesting theory, Sol," Angel said, rubbing his nose. "I think I'll assign myself to do some research on that."

"Hey, Angel," Sol lowered his voice to almost a whisper, "if you was to meet my son, could you tell if he was on drugs? And what kind?"

Angel scratched his head. "Maybe. If it's not just for a minute. Even then, I could probably tell something. How long you figure it's been going on?"

Sol grunted. "I don't know if anything's going on. I just have a feeling. He's hardly ever in the house anymore. He's got nothing to say when he's there. He's like in another world, you know."

"He going to school?"

"Yeah." Sol sighed. "I check. I check every week or so.

He's there, most of the time, but Shel, I don't know, he was never one for books. It's a mystery. It's a terrible mystery."

Angel patted Sol on the shoulder. "Bring him around." And thought: "He's right. Jews ain't what they used to be."

The *New York Post* truck drove up and a beefy man next to the driver slouched out and tossed a bound pile of papers on the ground next to the newsstand. Sol and Angel looked down at the headline:

BLONDIE THROWN OUT WITH THE GARBAGE

Angel shook his head. "Takes garbage to know garbage."

A tall, smooth black man stopped in front of them. "Gentlemen," he said, holding out the head shot of a dead blonde in her early twenties, "I'm Detective Dickerson, Ninth Precinct. Have you seen her around at all? Recently, or not so recently?"

"She the one in the garbage?" Sol kept his hands away from the picture.

"Yeah, you got it."

"No," Sol said. "I never saw her."

Angel took the photograph from Dickerson, looked at it closely, and shook his head. "Seen some like her, but not her."

"You sure?" the detective asked.

Angel looked at him. "I wouldn't swear. But she doesn't bring anything to mind."

Dickerson handed out two cards. "If either of you remember anything, or hear anything, let me know."

Sol cut the twine, picked up the *Post*s, and placed them on the stand. "Is it true you still haven't found the rest of her?"

Dickerson smiled. "That'll be a lot harder to identify."

"You mean," Sol was genuinely disturbed, "it wouldn't

be just a match-up? There's small parts of her body all over the place?"

"Who knows? said the detective. "This isn't Dayton, Ohio, you know. You never know what you're going to get here."

10

That evening, around eight, Dickerson was staring at a short, thickset man in his seventies halfway down the block on East Fifth Street between Avenues C and D. He had not appeared to move during the hour or so that Dickerson and Green had been showing the photograph of the recently deceased to anyone they could find at home or nesting in a doorway.

"Is that a piece of sculpture?" Dickerson asked his partner.

"That's Moishe. Moishe Kagan. Used to be an organizer with the Garment Workers, the ILG. Retired. Moishe's been retired too long, much too long. These guys, they got no place to go in the morning anymore. After a while, some of them just stand in the street, like statues, like Moishe."

Dickerson looked at the statue again. "Can he take care of himself?"

"Oh yeah. He's got all his marbles. But he's got nothing to use them for anymore. I heard he's got cancer. But with him, that'll take forever too."

"He live alone?"

"His wife left him," Green said.

"She picked a lousy time to do it."

Green smiled. "She left him fifty years ago. Moishe used to tell me, 'You taste something once and it gives you heartburn, you don't try it again.' He's lived alone ever since."

27

"Why'd she leave him?"

"Talk to him sometime. His charm will knock you over."

The two detectives turned up Avenue C to flash the photographs in stores and on the lively street corners where vivid young men grinned fiercely at gawkers in cars stopped for a red light.

Back around the corner, Moishe had not moved. His large blue eyes, under a mass of white bangs, seemed to be staring at a tall, gloomy abandoned building, all alone in a field of shattered bricks, glass, and excrement.

"She had a waist," Moishe Kagan was saying very softly, "so small you were afraid to hold it too hard, it would break. And the hair. So black, like, like a panther. Aiy, the eyes were—what? Green. What else? And the perfume, always the same perfume. Not pleasant, to tell the truth. Sharp, a little sour. But you looked at the waist and the little tush, who cared about the perfume? I bet you she's fat and smells bad now no matter how much of that perfume she pours on. And I'd have to live with that."

The statue laughed, also softly.

"You don't want to stay out much longer, do you, Moe?" the large black uniformed cop said to him gently.

"You a nurse?" Moishe Kagan looked up at the policeman, baring his teeth. "Funny, you don't look like a nurse. I'm not breaking a law standing here, am I? Tell me. Give me the law. You got a complaint from somebody? Who? Or is this maybe a ghetto, I'm not allowed out after a certain hour. Hah? Are you my keeper, is that it?"

The cop brushed his hands together. "Okay, Moe, okay. Sleep well."

"Good night, nurse," the old man snapped.

11

"**W**ant a date?" Two hours later, a slender black woman in her late twenties, standing in a doorway at the corner of Fourth Street and Avenue B, smiled at Moishe Kagan and showed tiny teeth. She wore tight green pants and a yellow halter.

Kagan stopped. "Turn around," he said.

"Feels *good*," she said as she turned her back on him, a hand on her thin, firm buttocks.

"Just touching and holding is all I want," the old man said, his voice a little hoarse. "I don't want to do nothing inside. You keep your clothes on."

"Whatever you say, handsome."

"How much?"

"For all night, I'll give you a special."

"I don't need all night. Inside there, but all the way in the back, I need maybe a minute. At most, two."

She laughed. "You sure do know what you want and how you want it. Okay, twenty dollars."

"Turn around," the old man said.

"Come on, you've already . . ."

"It's not for that."

Shaking her head, she turned her back as Moishe loosened his belt, put his hand into his undershorts, pushed aside his stiff penis, pulled out some bills, put twenty dollars between his teeth, returned the rest to his shorts, pulled up his pants, tightened his belt, cupped a hand under her behind, and sighed, "Here's the money. Let's go in there.

"You know," Moishe Kagan told the young black woman a few minutes later, "you people—I don't mean you black people, I mean you prostitutes—get a bad rap. Like you're worse than scum. The truth is," the old man was shaking his finger at her, "you perform a service that gives pleasure. How many so-called decent people," his voice rose, "make their living giving other people pleasure?"

She looked at Moishe Kagan with puzzlement verging on alarm.

The old man, jabbing a finger into her shoulder, continued. "You should be *proud* of what you do. Bringing pleasure is a good thing. What my people call a *mitzvah*. I mean, a woman these days becomes a lawyer and goes into a corporate law firm that works for landlords or Con Edison, and whom does she screw? She screws the workingman, and her screwing does not bring the workingman any pleasure. To say the very least. Yet *she* gets respect and *you,* you people get looked at like you got a disease. Which maybe you have, but that's the fault of your working conditions in this capitalistic society. It is not *your* fault."

"Gee," the black woman's tongue lingered over her tiny teeth, "that makes a lot of sense, you know that? A lot of sense. Tell you what? I want to do something for you. Whatever you want. No charge."

"Let me give you a tip, young lady," Moishe Kagan roared. "A great principle of trade unionism—the greatest and most basic principle of trade unionism—is DO NOT EVER GIVE YOUR LABOR AWAY. YOUR LABOR IS ALL YOU HAVE IN THIS WORLD."

"Not even for a friend?" she ran a thin finger down Moishe's cheek.

"You start giving it away," Kagan shook the finger off, "and soon all you will have is *schnorrer* friends sucking around you. And no income. Remember what I tell you. And one other thing. You should put a mint or something in your mouth before each job."

12

Around nine the next morning, Chief Mulvaney was on the phone, being interviewed for a *Sunday News* article on the Internal Affairs Division.

"They are called field associates," the Chief patted the new, butter-smooth, deep brown leather briefcase on his desk. "They are police officers who act as our eyes and ears where they work. They report to us when they have reason to suspect police corruption or any other wrongdoing in the department. No, my dear, the associates get no extra pay for this work. They do it because they are honest, and they want to be part of an honest force.

"Yes," Mulvaney put his feet on the desk, "nobody knows who they are, including their commanders. Only a very, very small number of people here at IAD know their identities." He stared, frowning, at a flaw in the leather. "Well, I'm not going to tell you how many associates we have, except to say that they're in every precinct and in most of the bureaus. Suffice to say, my dear, every cop lives in justified fear that every other cop may be with the IAD.

"You're right again. The field associates are in addition to our full-time IAD investigators. No, the associates themselves are never asked to testify against other cops. Their names *never* become public. In all the time I've been here, fourteen years and four police commissioners, no one has ever discovered the identity of a single field associate. We are very, very careful about that."

Mulvaney looked at his assistant, Jeremy, who had just come into the office and placed a batch of unopened mail on the Chief's desk. "What did you say?" Mulvaney sat up straight and glared at the phone. " 'Every American, including cops, has a right to face his accusers.' "

Jeremy, turning away from the Chief, snickered.

"Let me tell you something, sister," Mulvaney spoke coldly into the phone. "Down here, we don't look at it like that. The accusers are not anonymous to *us*. Look, our concern is the information we get. Is it true? Or is it false? But don't think the accused doesn't get due process. The Patrolmen's Benevolent Association wouldn't have it any other way. They provide every cop we investigate with a lawyer and each one of those lawyers, believe me, is dedicated to the proposition that every cop, from time immemorial, is innocent of everything. So they get a lawyer, and they get due process. But if we get the goods on them, they go. They get put away. Okay, my dear? You got any more questions, call anytime."

Chief Mulvaney hung up. "You know, Jeremy, it's like a goddamn disease. Rights! Everybody got to have all the rights coming to them, and then some. Blacks, fags, cripples, even the goddamn Chinese are yelling for their rights. They don't want a prison down here. You got to walk on eggshells with everybody. And now this broad tells me it's unconstitutional if crooked cops don't get to see their accusers. The next thing they'll tell me, Jeremy, is that I can't bug your office without letting you know."

The Chief roared in self-appreciation as Jeremy, clucking amiably, waited until Mulvaney had subsided and then said, "Our alumnus, Mr. Dickerson, is well thought of in the Ninth Precinct. Pulls his weight, doesn't keep reminding you he's black all the time, and is now working with Noah Green while Green's partner, Sam McKibbon, is on vacation. Our man could not be in a better position."

Mulvaney lit a cigarette. "Have Dickerson come around."

"I've already arranged that. Tomorrow at three. I checked your calendar."

"Good. Tell me about Green."

"Not to be believed." Jeremy leaned against the wall. "The son of a bitch is so decent that some of our regular customers ask for him to confess to. I kid you not. On the other hand, he never gives up on a case. He is Inspector Javert converted to Judaism and cheap cigars. He smokes Robert Burns, can you believe it? He has the best clearance rate in the precinct."

"Does he take anything?"

"Chief, there's not even a whisper. He's got a record in all respects that they should bronze and put on the wall of the Police Academy."

"What does he do when he's not being an example to all of us?"

"Divorced and remarried a year ago. Just had a kid. His wife is a reporter, Shannon Leahy, from *The Post*."

"Yich!" Mulvaney got up and walked to the window. "She an Australian?"

"Boston, Chief. A *landsman* of yours. And some looker, they tell me. Twenty years younger than Green."

Mulvaney rubbed an eye. "Sounds like they're both from the KGB. So there's nothing?"

"Chief, maybe it's a waste of time to follow up on that note."

"Maybe. Maybe not. It all looks too kosher. No, my boy, we're going ahead. If Mr. Green is all you say, he has nothing to fear."

"Except fear itself."

"The force never promised anyone a rose garden, Jeremy."

13

With Jeremy out of the room, the Chief began to sort his mail from the outside world. In one pile, he gingerly placed all the handwritten letters and the few typed ones that appeared to have been executed by citizens rather than institutions. The rest he poured into the buttery new briefcase to be read, at one time or another, before he went home at seven or eight or perhaps nine. It was Mulvaney's rule never to bring any work home.

"You've got to have a few hours," he would tell Jeremy every once in a while, "to clear your mind of all this shit." And so, at home in Gramercy Park, after dinner, he and his wife, Mary Lou, would go into the library and listen to Haydn, Mozart, Boccherini, Scarlatti, and on holidays, Charles Ives and the Clancy Brothers. Once a week, after the concert, there would be champagne, and the Chief would take Mary Lou upstairs to bed. On the other nights, after the concert, he stayed up alone for an hour more, reading the Boston papers. He liked to stay in touch with the hometown.

Some nights, of course, the Chief's retreat would be pierced by one or more phone calls. Jeremy, for instance, with news of a field associate terrified of being found out by his feral colleagues. It was indeed true that although not a single field associate had been exposed during Mulvaney's tenure, a number of other cops, inaccurately believed to be volunteer snitches for IAD, had felt the displeasure of the boys, and some of the girls, in their precinct. For example, everything in their lockers tossed out the window. Followed by the lockers. The tires of their cars most foully assaulted. And in one or two of the more indelicate precincts, excrement of uncertain origin on the front seat of said cars. There had also been phone calls at home, with some child being told to tell his dad to watch himself at all times.

When this sort of thing happened in a precinct, the real field associate would sometimes get nervous to the point of panic. It was then that the Chief would get a call from Jeremy, sigh, blow a kiss to Mary Lou, and leave the house to meet the apprehensive associate on a quiet street, in a precinct far from the one in which he worked or lived.

Just the two of them. In most cases, the associate, after an hour or so, would apologize to the Chief for his skittishness and would pledge even more devotion to keeping the force clean. Most of the associates who stood fast were single. It was harder for some of the married associates to bring the pressure home with them and keep it locked in. Mulvaney understood and told the relatively few who insisted on leaving his service that their work had been greatly appreciated and now they had only their own noses to keep clean.

The only other evening interruptions, and they were rare, had to do with the IAD's taking in of a cop utterly caked with corruption but stonily unwilling to admit a blessed thing. Some of those hard nuts became harder through the night, and when not even the slightest crack showed by the small hours, the Chief was called. From his days as a homicide detective, Mulvaney was known throughout the department as being able to make a stone sing. Without raising his voice, or his hand.

"And did he tell you what you wanted to know?" Mary Lou would invariably ask the Chief next morning.

"Indeed, he did, the poor mistaken lad."

"And how," the stern-faced lady would say, smoothing the Chief's silver hair, "did you ever get him to tell you?"

"The easiest way in the world, Mary Lou," the Chief would say, spreading marmalade on his English muffin. "I simply laid out the options he had, and let him choose. The most attractive one was to blubber out his guilt and tell us the names of all the other cops involved in the corruption."

"Why was that the most attractive option?"

"Because otherwise, he would be going away for a very long time, and I told him stories, some of them with pictures I happen to have, of cops who became convicts and what happened to them in the general population when the lights went out. If he sings, however, he will be a special wing and only for a reasonably short time, and watched all that time. By us. The picture that really does the job is one of that fellow, Hanrahan, in 'sixty-seven, who had his balls cut off in Dannemora."

"Oh, Wilfred!"

This morning, in his office, the Chief, smiling in remembrance of these satisfying dialogues with Mary Lou and with the poor mistaken lads, slid a letter from the pile in front of him with a fingernail, held it down with that fingernail, and slit it open with a penknife in his other hand. The letter read:

THE CORRUPTION IN THE NINTH PRECINCT IS FESTERING. DETECTIVE NOAH GREEN BROKE BREAD WITH CRIMINAL LAWYER JASON MENDELSSOHN AT GUDAITIS BAR AND GRILL, 125 ESSEX STREET, LAST THURSDAY AT 1:00. THEY WERE NOT THERE FOR THE CUISINE.
YOU WOULD DO WORSE THAN TO FOLLOW IN THE FOOTSTEPS OF THOMAS BYRNES.

FROM ONE OF HIS ADMIRERS.

The Chief laughed, and then laughed some more, so loudly, Jeremy knocked to see if he could share the joke.

"Come in, come in," Mulvaney said, still chortling. "Read the letter on the desk."

Hands in pockets, Jeremy did just that.

"Imagine," said the Chief, "that motherfucker telling me about Thomas Byrnes. Ever hear of him? Of course, you haven't. This department neglects the teaching of history. Just like the public schools. All right. Inspector Thomas Byrnes. Came from Ireland as a child. Joined the force during the Civil War, made captain, took charge of the Detective Bureau in 1880, and turned it into a real one, the first professional detective bureau this city ever had. Byrnes was raised to Inspector. He was known for his devilish ability to look at a man once and know all there was to know about him. And he never forgot anyone. He was also known, as one of his colleagues said, for his skill at being all things to all men, as circumstances demanded.

"Thomas Byrnes had a daughter." The Chief was now slowly walking around the room. "The daughter married a Fitzgerald, and the Fitzgeralds had a daughter who married a Mulligan, and the Mulligans had a daughter who married a Mulvaney, and the Mulvaneys had a son. This very lad." He bowed.

Pointing at the letter on his desk, Mulvaney said, "It is our friend's intent to shame me in front of my ancestors." He laughed. "If this faceless bastard could find out that much about *me,* the odds are, Jeremy, that he may know something about this Noah Green."

14

As Mulvaney was paying his respects to Inspector Thomas Byrnes at One Police Plaza, in the third-floor living room of a brownstone on Twelfth Street, between Fourth and Third Avenues, Detective Noah Green, in deep astonishment, sat on a window seat looking at a long, lean, red-haired woman in her early thirties nursing a baby.

His baby. *His* woman, for Crissake. Incredible. Ten years from retirement and all of a sudden, as if he'd rubbed a lamp he'd found on the street, and pleaded:

"Genie, who will take care of me when I am old? Who will take care of me *now?* Genie, make me a family!"

Delighting in the wonderment of it all, Green walked to the woman and kissed her on the back of the neck. Shannon turned and stroked his cheek. "If you weren't so rude to reporters, this would never have happened."

Green spread his hands in innocence.

"Sure," his wife went on. "That homicide in the Village. You were so nasty. 'Damn it,' I said, 'I'll cut *him* down to size.' And now look at you."

"Well," Green said, "it's a question of who did what to whom."

Bending over the infant, Shannon began to sing in a clear contralto, with just enough vibrato to touch the soul:

> *One day a mother came to a prison*
> *To see an erring, but precious son.*

> *She told the warden how much she loved him.*
> *It did not matter what he had done.*

The child's tiny fist reached up to Shannon.

"Where the hell did you get that?" Green asked.

"Me father. He knew all kinds of songs, not just Paddy songs. No matter where they came from, he loved them all—so long as they had the truth in them."

"You're telling Max here," Green walked over and stooped, staring at the baby, "that he can do whatever he damn well pleases and Mama will love him all the same. He can rape and murder and bash babies against the wall, and Mama will—"

"You got it, buster," Shannon grinned at her husband. And sang again to the child:

> *She did not bring him parole or pardon.*
> *She brought no silver or gold.*
> *It was a halo bright, heaven's light,*
> *The sweetest gift—a mother's smile."*

"Oh shit," the detective said.

> *She left a smile, son, you can remember.*
> *She's gone to heaven, from heartaches free.*
> *The bars around her could never change her.*
> *You were her baby, and ere will be."*

The baby was crying.

"See," Shannon smiled at the boy, "he's learned to be guilty before he's done anything. That'll keep him out of trouble all his life."

"The guilt comes from my genes," Green said. "Well, I got an hour."

"Indeed." She was starting to change the baby's diaper. "Time for his nap, right?"

"His, yes."

"Listen, if you don't want to."

"Is that how you go about being a cop? 'Listen, if you don't want to tell me you did this terrible thing, you don't have to. Oh no. I, Detective Noah Green, would never force myself on anybody. Oh no. I am a saint. My wife is a saint. And this baby is immaculate. Oh yes."

Detective Green kissed his wife on the back of her neck and placed his hands firmly, very firmly, on her hips.

"Unhand me," Shannon said as she placed the baby in the bassinette. "You've not read me my rights."

He moved his hands up and around her waist. "You have none when it's hot pursuit."

She turned her head to stick out her tongue. "I didn't tell you, did I? I joined the Civil Liberties Union. You'll be hearing from them. This is state action, it is, what your hands are doing."

He dropped his hands. "You haven't? You haven't joined the Civil Liberties Union?"

"I have not," Shannon smiled. "And I am insulted that you would think for a moment that I would. Hell, I've had to interview their president, more than once, and some of the board members. Yech! They act like their shit doesn't smell."

Green looked pained.

"Sorry, I forgot I was a lady. And while they are looking at me in pity that my father the hod carrier never told me about the Constitution, and certainly my priest in the pay of Rome never did, they are so mean to each other. I was on a story, and I got hold of the minutes of some of their meetings. God, they gum each other half to death. Oh, I'll not be joining the likes of them in this life. Whited sepulchers they are, chirping about fairness while they put the shiv in each other's ribs. And what do they do after all? Force the schools to take back some yeggs they've suspended for more than sufficient reason. I'd like to see a judge say that those animals, instead of being pushed back into school, have to spend the year at the offices of the New York Civil Liberties Union. Yes, indeed. Hey—what are you doing?"

They were in their bed.

"Hey, don't you roll me over like that without asking."

15

A little past two o'clock the next morning, the wind was up, and on Avenue D and Fifth Street, there was no one in sight, a vista that made Angel nervous. "I'd rather see the mothers than feel them," he muttered to himself. But then, shrugging, Angel started scatting along with the rhythm section in his head that was playing "El Safacon de la 102nd Street," but that song of the garbage can made him remember something he didn't want to remember, so he changed the tune but kept staring at the cans he passed until, there it was. He wouldn't have noticed it if it hadn't been for that damn song, there it was, the tip, a little more than the tip, of a finger peeking out of a banana skin, under the tin cover.

"Oh no." Angel decided he could not stand seeing the vomit if he threw up so he didn't throw up. "What the hell is this? Am I Death's garbage man? Who put my name in? Do I get a break later on my own case? Shit!"

He sighed. "Okay, this time I'm not going to look all the way in." He sighed again. "That's a dark fingertip. Very dark. This is a killer that does not want to make black folks feel left out. If it's the same nut. But why should it be the same nut? There's got to be two, three hundred people walking these streets who'd cut a lady in half and throw the top of her in the garbage can. Probably more. Probably lots more."

Angel put out his hand to lift the cover of the garbage can

but smacked his hand down and couldn't help grinning, remembering Dr. Strangelove. He did this three times and finally, with a stick from the gutter, he pried the cover open just enough to see part of the way in.

Nestled on a bed of coffee grounds and eggshells was a thin black face, the face of a woman about twenty, wearing a yellow halter. Angel could follow her body down to her small waist, but from there on, all he could see was what the neighborhood had been eating for the past couple of days.

"Yeah," Angel said softly. "Sylvia. B and Fourth. She works that doorway. Worked. Sweet and stupid as they come. That was some unsatisfied customer. Hey, I saw an old guy pointing a finger at her, and yelling a couple of nights ago. The statue. The old Jewish fart. My friends," Angel looked down at several cats who had wandered by, "let me give you a sound piece of advice. Nobody is harmless."

With the stick, he pushed the garbage can cover back into place. "Okay, Mr. Detective Green, it is wakeup time. Death's garbage man is calling. Damn, if I keep finding these things, Noah's going to think I did it. Nah. Everybody loves Angel, everybody trusts Angel, because Angel is a good boy.

"Angel is a good boy because the temptations down here are so fucking tacky. So the question, gentlemen," he said to the audience of cats, which had grown larger, "could not be more simple. What is Angel's price? But will we ever know? This boy, this young man, could go all through his short life and never be sufficiently tempted to know his price and enjoy the proceeds thereof."

Angel suddenly had a vision of Sylvia coming out of the garbage can. Or at least the top of her. Whistling in search of a tune, Angel ran, looking for a phone booth that had a phone in it. Four blocks away he finally looked back. Nothing. Sylvia must have ducked behind a car.

16

Some eight hours later Captain Fortunato Randazzo was staring at his hands. "Anybody know any of her other customers?" he said without looking up. "The black one. That Sylvia."

"We found out there were a few regulars," Green said. "But no names, no nothing. She'd mostly go into their cars, their cheap Jersey cars. Moishe stood out. None of her other customers looked like Moishe. He says he only did it once, but once was enough to make him famous."

"He knows from nothing, right?" Randazzo asked his hands.

"Right," Dickerson stubbed out a cigarette. "All he knows is what her ass felt like."

"Don't be vulgar," Randazzo glared at Dickerson. "Especially now. This woman had a mother. You understand?"

Dickerson nodded.

"I didn't hear you," Randazzo rumbled.

"Yes, sir! I understand."

"You were talking without feeling," Randazzo said as he rose from his desk. "It's a disease in this business. It gets in the way of the work. A cop who sees these people, whatever they've done, as having been human, as having had mothers and fathers and what not, he will do a better job. *Farshteyst?*" He looked at Green.

"Did I ever say no?" Green said.

"She was a big user," Dickerson lit another cigarette.

"Horse?" Randazzo asked.

"Horse, whatever. Give her airplane glue, she'd groove on that."

"Okay," Randazzo slapped his desk. "The connections? We got any connections between Blondie and Sylvia?"

"Both whores," Green said. "Blondie has a number of names, the legit one is probably Marni Chambers. A solo practitioner, so far as we can tell. Upscale. She worked out of a dentist's office in the East Thirties. After hours. After his hours. It was in a professional brownstone, and she gave him a very nice taste every month. More than paid his rent. The only other thing we know so far is she was a junkie. She needed good stuff, regular, so she could keep herself in shape for the customers. No fun banging somebody who's sniffing and scratching all the time."

"Watch it," Randazzo frowned. "This Marni, she had a mother too."

"I figure she was killed here," Green went on, "because that's where her connection was. A lot of good stuff's been around lately. Anyway, we got a lot more canvassing to do, see if anybody knows her."

"Any connection between Blondie and Sylvia except that they're whores?" Randazzo was sitting on the edge of his desk.

"Not yet, except for the way they split," Green said.

Dickerson smiled. Randazzo did not.

"What else?" Randazzo snapped.

"If Marni had a list of customers," Green said, "and I'm sure she had some kind of date book, we haven't found it yet. The dentist, of course, is astounded by the revelation that she used his premises for illicit purposes. He says he thought she was running evening classes in how to pass the real-estate license exam. He says he knows nothing about her except that her checks didn't bounce. The dentist is a creep and a liar, but I don't think he was a partner. He's in deep mourning. All that lovely money every month gone."

"Sylvia," Randazzo said, "this Sylvia with whose first name you gentlemen are so familiar, she has a last name?"

"Robinson," Randall Dickerson said. "From Bed-Stuy. Mother dead. Cancer. Father unknown. Sylvia Robinson dropped out of school in the tenth grade. Busted for prostitution at least thirty-six times. That's all the computer gave us but that's not necessarily all the computer had. Fined each time. In the jug three times, same charge, but some judge wanted to prove something, God knows what. That's it. No violence, no stealing. Just a steady hooker."

Randazzo gloomily went for some sourballs in the large apothecary jar on his desk. "Could be a religious nut. God told him to send all the hookers to hell."

"Why cut them in half," Dickerson said, "and give us only the top?"

"So they can't do it no more, even in hell," Randazzo said, not smiling. "All right, let's see if any of God's little helpers have been let out lately by the fucking parole board. "You know something?" he looked at Green. "The more I steep in this cesspool, the more I am convinced there's got to be the death penalty for attempted murder, not just the times they bring it off. Way it is now a guy makes an attempt, you put him in for a few years, he gets out, he's still got killing in him. Chances are he'll try again, and sooner or later, bingo! A dog almost kills somebody, you shoot the dog. An animal's an animal. Four legs, two legs, what's the difference? You catch my drift?"

The Captain sighed, and stared at his hands again.

Green chewed on a cigar, and motioned to Dickerson to leave the office. When he had, Green said softly, "We've been working together a long time, Fortunato. So maybe I can say this. You don't look like yourself. You don't sound like yourself. Not for the last month or so. Maybe you need some time off?"

"I don't know," Randazzo looked past Green. "I don't know what it is. Yeah, I know what it is. You know what I like to do? I like to work in the garden. Gets my mind off all this shit. I got a little garden on the roof of the apartment house. Not supposed to have one there but is the landlord going to fuck with me? So this morning I go out to smell the flowers, touch them, so soft, softer than a baby, you know. Somebody's stepped on them, there's an empty pint of Mr. Boston gin, cigarette stubs, a condom, and a half-eaten apple. Right in my garden."

Randazzo shook his head. "I shoved the whole fucking mess into the incinerator, the garden too, it was part of the mess now. Tell me about evolution. A baboon wouldn't have done that. Now, listen, I want the statue to volunteer to tell you as much as he can remember about every whore he's been with as far back as he can remember."

"If Moishe's a suspect," Green said, "I'll have to—"

"Who said he's a suspect? You're beginning to hear things? Maybe you need some time off."

17

In the middle of that afternoon, Dennis, an old man with the look of a crooked walking stick, was standing behind the bar at Rafferty's on Seventh Avenue and Twenty-First Street. The establishment suffered transients but opened its pickled heart only to the regulars. Dennis, while reaching for a bottle of Gordon's gin, farted.

"Excuse me, Lieutenant," the barkeep turned his face to the cash register in embarrassment. "Another argument against free will."

Jeremiah Riordan, his billowing white hair reaching over the collar of his gray cardigan sweater, looked up from *Commentary.* "Excuse you for what?"

"Oh, for not freshening up your glass, Lieutenant."

"You'd be better off freshening up the air," Riordan smiled his lizard's smile. "But yes, I can do with another." He looked at his watch. "I always hated waiting. That's the bad part of having one of them after all this time. I've been used to waiting for no one, except some animal when we were on a stakeout."

"But I bet you it's not all that bad, having one?" Dennis rubbed his hands together underneath the bar and did a slow waltz step on the way to the bottle of Gordon's. "She's a lady, and a stunner too."

"She's no stunner." Riordan looked at Dennis with his ice-blue eyes. "She's not a dog, but nobody would mistake her for Jean Harlow. What I like about her is she's no dummy. Got a good, sly mind." Riordan drank the double gin in one gulp, and then took a sip of the water chaser. "And she knows how to put it in," Riordan cackled. "That's an art, you know. Most women are fumblers."

Reading on, Riordan started to shake his head, making growling noises deep in the back of his throat. "God damn it!" he banged his fist on the bar. "Dennis! Do you know who runs the government of the United States?"

"Yes, I do," Dennis snapped to. "Whoever runs the government of Israel runs the government of the United States."

"And what is the reason for the subjugation of this nation to a foreign power?"

"The Jewish lobby has captured Congress."

"That guy Green ever come in anymore since he went down to the Ninth Precinct?" Riordan asked casually.

"Once in a while. He's not a bad guy for a—"

"Dennis," Riordan pointed to his glass, "you are tottering on the edge of your grave and you still haven't learned that they're all the same. In all of history, not a single Hebrew has merited the trust of a Christian. Not one."

The barkeep frowned in concentration, opened his mouth, shut it again, and then said, "Well, what about Jesus?"

"Really, now." Riordan got off the bar stool and leaned over the bar until his forefinger was tapping Dennis' Adam's apple. "Do you remember the man with the withered hand, the withered right hand?"

"Can't say that I do."

"It was in the synagogue on the Sabbath. Jesus was there, and Jesus saw this man with the withered hand. Watching Jesus were the scrimy scribes and the scrimy Pharisees muttering. Would he work on the Sabbath, this Jesus? Would he cure on the Holy Day? If he did, ah-ha!, they'd have him as a bad Jew. Now what did Jesus do? You don't know, so don't answer. He said to the man with the withered hand, 'Stand up. Move up here.' And Jesus said to the stinking Jews watching his every move, 'Is it against the law on the Sabbath to do good? Is it against the law on the Sabbath to save life?' Then Jesus said to this suffering man, 'Stretch out your hand.' A moment later, it was not withered any longer.

"But the Jews were furious. Snarling among themselves, plotting to destroy this man who didn't give a damn for the Jewish law if it got in the way of his helping someone. So," Riordan gulped down half of his newly filled glass, "how can you say, Dennis, that Jesus was a Jew when he was the *enemy* of the Jews. Whoever he was born to, Jesus was not a Jew as Jews define Jews. That's why they spit whenever they hear his name. It's time you knew that too, Dennis. Even Jewish children spit when they hear his name."

"Well now," Dennis turned his back so that he could swiftly pick his nose, "I never thought of it that way."

"Green, he ever come in with anybody?" Riordan asked.

"Oh, are you on a case, Jeremiah? Has someone given you a case?" Claire's throaty voice spun Riordan around.

"Yes," he hissed. "The President himself woke me up this morning. Six-thirty it was. Could I undertake a very secret and dangerous assignment for the good of the country? I could, and I am. And that's all I'll ever tell you about it."

"How exciting!" Claire said as she bounced onto the stool next to his. "But one thing you *can* tell me. How *is* President Roosevelt? Is he getting enough sleep with all the cares on him, and the braces and all?"

"To hell with you, Mary Lou!" Riordan laughed. "And the Jews too!"

"And the Jews too!" came the echo from Dennis.

"Well," said Claire, "I'll have to think about that a little."

18

Early that evening, standing behind his desk, Chief Mulvaney smiled broadly, extended his hand to the tall, crisp, black detective, and said, "Appreciate your coming by, Randall."

The detective shook his hand swiftly. "Anybody ever refuse one of your invitations?"

Mulvaney chuckled. "Oh, they all come, eventually. Some get lawyers who tell them they don't have to come, but they all come. Now, it's been how long since you were so good as to help us?"

Dickerson looked at the manila folder in front of the Chief, saw his name on the right-hand corner, and decided to play the game. "About nine years ago. You put me in the Two-Three right out of the Academy."

"Yes, indeed," Jeremy, who was sitting on a couch across from the Chief, said, his bright eyes glistening. "I remember the first one of yours up there. There were two cops shaking down the convenience ladies, and banging them for free, of course, and then arresting them anyway, of course. Who'd take their word against a cop's? So there was never a complaint."

"How'd you know about it?" the Chief asked Dickerson.

The detective glanced again at the folder in front of the Chief. "I was going with the sister of one of those ladies. The sister I was going with was not in the profession."

"She was a secretary at *El Diario*," Jeremy said idly.

"Proofreader," Dickerson corrected him.

"When we got those cops in East Harlem," Mulvaney lit a cigarette, "did your stomach turn over a little? Ratting on your buddies."

"First time's supposed to be the hardest," Dickerson said, "but it wasn't that hard. I kept remembering the talk you gave at the Police Academy. A bad cop makes all cops look bad, you said. A bad cop leaves each one of us more alone out there, you said. Why would a civilian want to help a cop if the chances were he was crooked, you said. So I was ready when you asked me to be an associate, just before I got out of the Academy. That's why I called Jeremy here when the lady I was going with told me what the guys in Two-Three were doing."

The Chief looked at Dickerson. "The time you turned in your partner—he was on the pad in at least four after-hours joints—did that bother you?"

"Hell, no. No way his partner couldn't have known, so if I didn't turn him, I'd have been burned because one of your boys would have turned me in too."

Mulvaney tapped his nose with his finger. "If you had a relative on the force, would you give him to us?"

"How close?"

"Brother. Brother you liked."

"No."

Mulvaney smiled. "I have a brother I'd turn in, but he's not on the force. All right, there came a time when, after you had been of considerable value to us, I offered you a place in the IAD. Full-time down here. You turned it down."

Dickerson folded his hands. "I don't mind going after bad cops part of the time, but not all of the time. That's not why I became a cop. I became a cop because there are a lot of bad cats out there in the street, civilian cats."

"Okay," the Chief nodded. "So we made you a detective."

"Helped make him a detective," Jeremy said.

"Sure, helped," Mulvaney winked at Dickerson. "I've assumed no one ever found out you'd been a field associate while you were at the Two-Three. But still, one never knows, do one? When you got your shield, I told you to give me a call if you ever had any trouble. You never called."

Dickerson shrugged. "Never had need to."

"But you never called with any more information, either."

Dickerson laughed. "Come on, everywhere I've been since, you've had field associates. You've had them in the toilets, for Christ sake."

The Chief and Jeremy leaned forward. "You knew who they were?" they said in chorus.

"Naw," Dickerson grinned. "Relax, I mean, captains got transferred, detectives started singing to grand juries. I got the picture. I figured you didn't need me."

"But if we have moles everywhere, Randall," the Chief said, "why have we sent for you now?"

"I been wondering about that," the detective said. "Especially since the Nine looks to be as clean as can be. And if there's something I'm missing, you've got somebody down there anyway. So what do you need me for?" He frowned. "Unless—"

"You got it," the Chief said.

"Aw come on," Dickerson shook his head. "You think you got something on Noah Green and because I'm his partner—"

"We've had some information," the Chief said.

"Anonymous, I bet," Dickerson grimaced.

"Oh, there's something wrong now with leads that don't come with a name and a picture? You don't accept anonymous tips yourself anymore? You just hang up on them?"

Dickerson put up his hands, as if in surrender.

"Here," Mulvaney handed the detective Xeroxes of the two notes about Noah Green.

Dickerson read them and, expressionless, read them again. "This all you got?"

"No," Mulvaney leaned back in his chair. "Now we got you. Do we?"

"I haven't changed my mind," Dickerson said. "When a bad cop shits, he shits on us all. I think you're dead wrong about this guy, but I've been fooled before. Just a few times, but then I guess you have too."

"Never," Mulvaney said. "I've been a bit premature at times perhaps, but never ultimately wrong."

"What's my code name?" Dickerson asked.

"John Lewis, as nondescript as they come," Jeremy said.

Dickerson rose, as did the other two.

"We really do appreciate this, Randall," the Chief held out his hand. "Welcome home."

"You don't have to make the bed," the detective said. "If anything's going down, I'll know it pretty quick. One thing. If you put one of your boys on me to see how I'm doing, I'll break his face. I don't like to be crowded."

Wilfred Mulvaney smiled and patted Dickerson on the shoulder. "Take care, young man. And watch out for innocent bystanders. You surely don't want to break any of their faces."

19

The next day, at about two, the thin, straight-backed elderly black man sat at the end of the bar on Avenue A and Twelfth Street, reading the Op-Ed page of *The Times*. In front of him was a glass of club soda.

Angel, bouncing through the door, waved at the bartender, hopped on a stool three spaces away from the black man, and ordered a Budweiser. Fishing through the pocket of his green corduroy jacket, Angel took out a paperback of *Bleak House*; a red marker pen, and a bedraggled notebook.

The black man glanced at the youngster and at the book, passed a finger over his lower lip several times, and without turning toward Angel, said into space, "That's the only one of his novels, you know, in which a woman is the narrator."

Angel, turning with a smile, raised his glass of beer. "I didn't know that! This is only the second one of his I've been reading. Boy, once you get into it, you can't get enough of it. And you know what I really like. There's no fooling around about who's good and who's bad. You know who you want to win, and you know who you want to *d-i-e-e-e!*"

This thin black man said to his glass of club soda, "Why did you follow me, young man?"

Angel smiled in some embarrassment. "God damn, I thought I was better than that. Well, it was curiosity, that's all. I mean, I see you around a lot, and nobody knows anything about you, and well, the main thing was I wanted to see if I could do it. I read some of those detective books,

but you don't know if *you* can do it until you do it, right?"
Angel took his beer and moved to the bar stool next to the
black man.

"How would you like it, young man," he turned his thin,
deeply lined, impassive face to Angel, "if someone followed
you? You think that's right, crowding a man like that,
poking into his business. And you not even a cop. Or are
you?"

Angel, laughing, shook his head. "I go to school. Finish-
ing up at Stuyvesant. Then I'm going to City. City College.
Then I'm going wherever I want to go. Look, I apologize. I
really do. I didn't think about how you might feel about it.
But you're right. I wouldn't want anybody doing it to me."

The black man motioned to the bartender, and pointed to
Angel's glass and to his own, "What did you find out about
me?"

"You were a court reporter for, like thirty-eight years,
and now you're a messenger. And you never make a mistake. That's what everybody told me, Mr. Fitzgerald."

The elderly black man stared at Angel. "If we're going to
know each other at all, young man, you keep calling me Mr.
Fitzgerald. One thing I notice about you is that you're much
too familiar."

"Whatever you say," Angel said, sliding off the stool.
"Whatever you say, Mr. Fitzgerald. "Hey, you got any
children? Nobody I asked knew."

"Nobody you asked *would* know," Fitgerald said as he
went out the door.

"Poor kids, if he ever had them," Angel said to the
bartender. "They'd have to learn not to be too familiar."

20

Moishe Kagan, in the evening of the day, was about to take his after-dinner shuffle. Locking the door of his second-floor, one-bedroom apartment on Seventh Street, between Avenues A and B—one third of the rent contributed by his son Balfour, the business manager who used to be an accountant—Kagan walked down the steps, and stopped.

Why should I care about B'nai Rappaport. First of all, what kind of name is that for a shul? It's the name for a dry goods store. Second, I have not been inside a shul since—since when? Since Millstein's grandson was bar mitzvahed. What, twenty years ago? How could I refuse Millstein? All the picket lines we walked. All the bosses we wished on they should go to ten different specialists and not one should know what the matter is with them.

So two months after the bar mitzvah, Millstein died. Think how terrible I would have felt if I had refused him one Saturday morning in shul for his grandchild. That was some shul! Rose windows. And the Torah! A Torah for the Rothschilds.

Kagan stood, a statue, on the sidewalk.

But B'nai Rappaport was, well what do you want, it was for the working class. The sweatshop class. A little place, on Stanton Street, no? Just looking in the windows before they boarded them up, I could see they were piece workers, whoever started that shul. Except for the rose windows, and they were nothing like those in Millstein's shul, nothing was ever finished, I mean finished. But you know what gets me? The note on the door. What was it: two, three years ago? The note that said, "Sorry, very bad news to notify that your synagogue closed because no helping hands given."

Moishe lowered his head.

"Your synagogue." When was it ever my synagogue? I was only in there once. I know, I know, it could have been mine. If I ever needed it. For what would I ever need it? Bastards. They didn't ask very far for helping hands. I got nothing else to do. I could have done something. But nobody told me. Schmucks. They put the note on the door when it's too late. What good is it now, except to make me feel bad?

Kagan started to walk slowly toward Avenue A, but there was a man in his path. A tall, very thin, very light-skinned Negro. To himself, Kagan still used Negro. As he used to say to himself, if Negro was good enough for Brother A. Philip Randolph, it was good enough for Moishe Kagan.

Through his white bangs, Kagan looked more closely at the Negro who was smiling at him. The smile of Hitler, if Hitler had been a mulatto. Kagan moved a step sideways, and the Negro moved a step sideways, still blocking him. "So?" Kagan said, "I'm not such a good dancer."

"Would you explain to me, Jew, why you are walking the streets?" Arthur said in a voice as soft as the evening breeze. "Jews are now legally entitled to kill black women, is that it?"

"Why would I kill her? I was jealous of her? She wouldn't give me a refund? What are you talking about? You don't know what you're talking about. And who are you anyway?"

Arthur looked down at Kagan. "God, listening to you talk is like listening to somebody throw up. Jew, you're being watched. All the time."

"You would do better going to a movie."

"You don't have much time left, Jew, and we have picked how you are going to die. You are going to die of being afraid, of being more afraid than you can stand, than anyone can stand, that's how you're going to die."

Kagan took a White Owl from a shirt pocket. "Tell me, why are you so sure I killed that poor young woman?"

"Because you're no ordinary customer. Look at you. A stinking old, old man. You must have wanted something from her so disgusting that she would rather die than do it with you."

"That's interesting," Kagan said. "What could it be? You've given me something to think about. Thank you. I hardly ever have new things to think about. Now, if you'll let me pass."

"Remember," Arthur said as he barely made some space on the sidewalk, "a life for a life. That's in *your* Bible."

"I'm not so good anymore at remembering," Kagan smiled at the Negro, "but every time I see dogshit on the street, I'll remember you."

Arthur pulled a long knife from a sheath inside his shirt, but the old man suddenly crouched, grabbed Arthur's balls, and twisted.

Gasping, Arthur fell on his knees.

"The last time I did that," Kagan said, standing over him, "was in Jersey. They hired some real *momsers*, worse than animals, much worse, to break up the picket line. One of them came after me with a hammer. Boy, did he have a look on his face, a murderer, just like you. I was young then, I think maybe I grabbed and twisted too hard. They told me he was never the same fellow. But that could only be an improvement."

Kagan walked past Arthur, stepping hard on the Negro's hand as he went.

Arthur looked after him, and grinned through his tears.

21

Once there had been a gas station on the corner of Avenue C and East Ninth Street, but now, in its ruins were just a charred sofa without any pillows, the carcass of a refrigerator, broken bottles, and on the freshly painted white wall, a mural—two bright green tendrils pointing to the black printed letters:

EN MEMORIA DE
ANA MERCEDES CRUZ
(FOURTEEN YEARS, NINE MONTHS)

Fortunato Randazzo forced himself, as every morning, to pass the mural on the way to his command at the Ninth Precinct. "God forbid I should come to work feeling good," he had once said to Noah Green. "Then the whole day would be an awful letdown. This way, I pay my respects to Ana Mercedes on the way here, and from then on I can't go anywhere but up."

Several months before, Ana Mercedes Cruz had been walking toward the corner of Avenue C and East Seventh Street one afternoon about four o'clock. She was on her way to get *The New York Post* for her father, who had been out of work so long that he was ashamed to go out into the street. As Ana Mercedes reached the corner, a self-employed man—his specialty was robbing drug addicts—aimed a gun at a junkie who was fleeing from him. The junkie ducked behind a car, and Ana Mercedes's head intercepted the bullet.

Ana Mercedes had been an unusually bright child, and was also noted for her good cheer. The priest had said she could become anything she wanted to be. He delicately neglected to say that the one exception was a priest. But Ana Mercedes never thought of that. She had wanted to work with the mentally retarded.

Her funeral was talked about for weeks after, so graceful had been the silver cars and so abundant the flowers. The neighborhood had pitched in to pay their last respects with children collecting door-to-door, and jars next to the cash registers in all the stores. But by far, the largest contributions were in cash, delivered to Ana Mercedes's father by respectful, restless young men who knew he understood they could not say who sent them.

The most remarkable part in the funeral had been the silence on the streets as the small coffin and its cortege slowly, very slowly, went by. Dealers, junkies, cops, children, women out shopping, all turned and froze as Ana Mercedes went to her reward.

Tears trickling down his face, a squat, middle-aged dealer—his operation was said to gross seventy-thousand dollars a day—promised himself the head of the animal who had killed this girl. His was not a mere sentimental promise of the moment, for it was widely believed that he had been responsible for the decapitated corpse found two weeks before at the bottom of an airshaft at East Sixth Street. The corpse had once been a vibrant Cuban, allegedly looking to relocate from Florida. The story was that the Cuban had walked into a meeting with the dealer, they had shaken hands, a vigorous handshake, and in the process, a tiny microphone had fallen out of the Cuban's ear. Later his whole head had left him.

The dealer went by many names, and no one knew which was rightly his. But most people in his employ called him

Mr. Chin, possibly because he had none, and also because although he was half-Chinese and half-German, he looked mostly Oriental, except for his snout.

The poor marksman who had kept Ana Mercedes perennially young in the memory of her friends and neighbors disappeared. The police put out queries and did a lot of canvassing, but mostly hoped for a phone call. The dealer, whose contract on the killer's head was reportedly for thirty thousand dollars, remained unfulfilled. And he remained greatly annoyed because no one had ever escaped from him before. In time, Mr. Chin was careful to avoid the mural in memory of Ana Mercedes because he had come to blame her for walking into the bullet in the first place and thereby causing him such frustration.

But Captain Fortunato Randazzo never missed a day of remembrance. Every morning, rain or shine, he stopped before the mural, gazed at it, shook his head, and cursed his fate that he should be spending the prime years of his life in a nightmare from which he could not shake himself awake. A nightmare in which the fat woman with the little-girl curls kept screaming at him at the Precinct Community Council meeting:

"If YOU lived here, if YOUR children had to live here, YOU wouldn't let these two-legged rats take over those buildings, take over the blocks, take over our lives, our LIVES! You can't walk the street without their trying to get you into one of those buildings! You can't walk the street, for God's sake, without being shot! Poor Ana Mercedes, poor Ana Mercedes. YOU, you police, what are you supposed to be here for if you can't protect a lovely innocent fourteen-year-old girl? Such a good girl. Gone, gone, because YOU don't know how to do your job!"

Randazzo had started to smile because of an instant image of a shotgun blast hitting that fat face with the little-girl curls. Biting his lower lip, he had said, "Madam, in the first five months of this year, we have made one thousand nine hundred eighty-seven arrests for drug trafficking on the Lower East Side. Double the number of arrests in the same period last year."

"How many of them are in jail, hah! How many of them are in jail, hah! What about THOSE numbers? What about THOSE numbers?" The voice, dark and harsh, belonged to a small man who owned a shoe store on Avenue A and looked as if he were made of black dust.

Captain Randazzo, with a massive attempt to keep his voice even, looked at the questioner, and said, "You are right, sir. Most of those arrested have not gone to jail, except for a few hours or a few days. But that is not our fault, sir. I would urge you to protest as vigorously to the judges and the prosecutors as you protest to us. More vigorously, because *we* are doing our job."

Just then, something happened to Fortunato Randazzo. Looking at those anxious, angry, bewildered faces, he had felt sick. Sick to his stomach sick to his heart. "Listen," he had said, holding out his arms and lifting his head, "we do not have the money to hire all the cops we need to clean out these bloodsuckers. And even if we *did* have the money," he was shouting now, "even if I could get a thousand new cops tomorrow, just for this precinct, and even if I had them here for a whole month, what would happen? Sure, I'd drive all the dealers and the steerers and the rest of them out of the neighborhood. For maybe six weeks. Then, then—they'd all be back. Unless I could keep those thousand cops forever."

"You mean there's no hope?" the fat lady yelled. "Is that what you're telling us?"

Randazzo sighed. He felt so sad, he wanted to hold her in his arms to comfort both of them. "Listen," he said. He spoke so softly that the room quieted down. "Listen, you know who the biggest employer is in this neighborhood. The dealers. You know how hard it is to get rid of something that so many people live off. We're going to keep on doing what we can. We're going to keep making arrests. A lot more arrests because we are getting more cops. Not a thousand, but a lot. The Mayor and the Police Commissioner are going to make this neighborhood an example. They're going to put the pressure on. But not forever. That's what I'm trying to tell you. We can't get rid of it forever. That's the truth, I'd be lying to you if I told you anything different."

Noah Green had been with Randazzo. "I hope there wasn't a reporter there," the detective said as they left the meeting. " 'Top Cop Throws in the Towel in War Against Drugs!' "

"I couldn't help it," Randazzo had said as they walked up the street. "I was getting mad at them for not believing my lies. That's crazy. They're grown-ups, so let them face the facts. They won't though. I did what I did for myself. I couldn't lie anymore. But they're going to keep demanding and demanding. Right now, they're writing letters to the Mayor and the Police Commissioner—demanding my head. I don't blame them. What a fucking way to live.

"Did you notice something?" He looked at Green and went on. "I bet you didn't notice. There was not one mention of the murders. Half a body popping out of a garbage can every once in a while doesn't scare them nearly so much as drugs. I understand, I understand. But Noah, I am fifty-two years old and I am in command of a precinct where murders, like garbage, are taken for granted. Noah, what did I do that God should despise me so?"

22

Late that afternoon, outside the Second Avenue Delicatessen the statue was listening to wedding music—a laughing clarinet, a strutting trumpet whose notes winked at you and elbowed you in the kishkes, an ecstatic trombone. *Klezmorim! Klezmorim! Play until we platz! But whose wedding is this? My own? Could it be? Yeah, she's dancing with her father.*

"Moishe," the big man with the face of a secondhand Saint Bernard said in his ear, "you shouldn't be outside by yourself. That guy's balls still hurt. He is bad news, Moishe, that Arthur. Stay in the house for a while. Or better yet, go visit your son."

With great reluctance, Moishe Kagan left the wedding and looked at Noah Green. "Who should I be outside *with*? You're going to give me a cop twenty-four hours a day? And my son, Balfour, if he wanted me to visit him, he'd tell me."

"Stay home then," Green said. "Watch television. This'll blow over. It's just that right now—"

The old man spat on the sidewalk. "Sonny, I don't live like a mouse. I never lived like a mouse. When David Dubinsky went out from the office and smashed those Communists over the head, who do you think was with him? Who do you think got hit so hard in the back, he was stooping like a hunchback for months? But the next time, still stooping like a hunchback, I went with a hammer, and it was like magic, sonny. I turned those rats into mouses.

66

Squeaking, squeaking, 'No more, please, no more!' One of them walked crooked for the rest of his rotten life. Another has the kind of nose it takes clowns a long time to put on."

Green shook his head. "Moishe, they'll come down Second Avenue in a car, and they'll blow your head off. No hammer, no nothing, will do you any good."

Moishe Kagan lifted his face to what was left of the sun. "So? So what am I supposed to do, Mr. Detective? I won't do it. Whatever it is, I won't do it. Whoever said, 'Live free or die'—I think it was Ben-Gurion—well, he was talking about me."

"One other thing," Green said, "if I weren't a cop, this wouldn't be any of my business, but how often do you do that, what you did with Sylvia?"

The old man laughed. "I saw her, it got hard, I mean hard. I figured it's been a long, long time, I could die tomorrow, why not do myself a favor now? If I don't get undressed, if I don't kiss her, I don't catch nothing, so what the hell? It was a passing fancy. She was selling, I was buying. That's all."

"How many times you done it with her?"

"That was it."

"And with others?"

"Sonny, I told you, it was a passing fancy. I've had a lot of passing fancies. This was the first one in years that didn't pass fast enough."

"Did you argue with her?" Green asked.

"About what?"

"About anything."

"Sonny," Moishe Kagan was becoming exasperated, "it was one-two-three-four-don't-slam-the-door. That's all. Argue? She liked it so much, she was going to give me one for free."

Green laughed. "You're a wonder, Moishe. A credit to your race. Listen, you remember Max Mendelssohn?"

The old man nodded vigorously. "Who could forget

Max? The best lawyer the ILG ever had. What a mean, vicious son of a bitch. Some of the best contracts we got because the bosses couldn't stand to negotiate with Max any more. Oi, what a mouth! He used to embarrass even me. Such a lovely man. When he died, I remember, we were all in a room, it was some kind of a meeting, when the phone call came, and Dubsinsky told us Max had gone. We were all crying, big, big tears. We were crying, until we were laughing.

"Everybody started remembering stories. Like when Max started, just out of some cockamamie law school in Massachusetts, he was working with those little pishers who were trying to organize the cap makers. And the bosses in those days, if they heard a word that somebody was even thinking of joining the union, 'OUT! THIS SECOND, OUT!' Until Max started coming around. You know what the bosses started calling Max? No, you wouldn't know, you're too young. The bosses started calling him, *Malakh Hamoves.*"

Green laughed. "The Angel of Death."

"You bet your ass, sonny boy, the Angel of Death. Nobody fucked with Max."

"Well, his son is a lawyer, too. Jason."

"I know," the old man said. "I read the papers. Big criminal lawyer. So?"

"So I told him about the girl that got killed. The black one."

"So?" Moishe said suspiciously.

"Moishe, it makes sense for you to have a lawyer while things are still fluid, you know. You're not a suspect, nobody's a suspect, but who knows what somebody will come up with, especially now that you're a champeen ball-twister. Moishe, somebody may try to do you in. Pin something on you. A good lawyer can stop that."

"What am I supposed to pay this Jason with, stories about his father?"

"He'll do it for nothing," Green said. "Because of his

father and the ILG. Here, here's his address and phone number."

The old man took the piece of paper, squinted at it, and put it in his shirt pocket. "Okay, when I have a chance."

"Moishe," Green put a hand on the old man's shoulder. "Go see him. Call him tomorrow."

Kagan looked at the detective. "You know something I don't know?"

"I know it never hurts to have a lawyer when nobody knows for sure what's going on. Moishe, you got nothing to lose."

The old man rubbed his nose. "One question. Since when does a cop tell somebody to get a lawyer?"

Green lit a cigar. "Where is it written that a cop is not a human being? My Uncle Alec had an ILG button that he wore on everything. His pajamas too, I think."

Kagan grunted. "So thank you. And thank your Uncle Alec. Stubborn as an ox, that man. He's dead, I suppose."

"Twenty years."

"Too bad. I was going to invite him to lunch one day at Ratner's. Just as well. We'd have gotten into a terrible fight about the ILG. Alec would be going on about how other unions should be half as good as ours, and I would be telling him how the ILG has come to stink from the head. Screwing the workers now that they're _schwartzes_ and Puerto Ricans and Chinese. Making deals with the Goddamn bosses. And your Uncle Alec would spritz me with the seltzer bottle, and I would pour the cream over his stupid head, and you know, it wouldn't be a bad time at all. I'm sorry the putz is dead."

"Moishe," Green said, "how the hell do you know whether Alec, whom you hardly knew in the first place, would disagree with you about where the union is now?"

Moishe grinned. "I know. Go prove me wrong."

23

"**S**o he banged Sylvia. Actually, he fondled her." Noah Green, the next afternoon, was leaning back in his chair in the squadroom. "But there's nothing to connect Moishe with the other one, Marni Chambers."

"We don't know," Randall Dickerson was sitting on the edge of the desk. "We don't know all of Marni's customers. We don't know if she did some work outside the brownstone."

"She wasn't a street hooker."

"She used to be." Dickerson pushed a rap sheet across the desk. "We finally got all of her out of the computer. I think it's all of her. Busy girl. And her real name is Sara. Sara Pearlstein."

"God damn," Green brought his chair down hard. "I thought I could always tell."

"How often does Kagan indulge?" Dickerson asked. "And where?"

"He says this was the first time in years. He's had passing fancies, he says, but this one didn't pass fast enough."

"You believe him?"

"Probably not," Green said. "He wouldn't want to admit any more of that than he was caught doing. To him it's unclean."

"To me too," Dickerson looked at Green. "Sara could have been doing some quickies down here, after she scored. Make up some of the bread. Before the brownstone, she used to work Chelsea—Eighth Avenue and thereabouts. Some of the ladies there say that Sara really liked street work. She liked to be surprised. Fondling would surprise her."

"Nobody's seen them together," Green said.

"What if it turns out somebody did?"

"You start thinking what-ifs and you bang right into the wall."

"I dunno," Dickerson said. "I got a hunch. Feels like a good one. I got a hunch your man, the statue, did them both in."

"Because they wouldn't join the union?"

"Something like that," Dickerson smiled.

"You're out of your fucking mind." Green walked out of the room.

24

"**Y**our partner already talked to me," the statue, placed in front of the furniture store, was looking at a man, across the street, picking a pair of pants out of a trash can, holding them up, nodding approvingly, and putting them over his arm. The ripe young woman beside him laughed and patted the seat of the pants.

"I know," Randall Dickerson said. "Just a couple of things. Won't take long."

"Well, I don't have to see the Governor until four, and I can skip the board meeting at Chase Manhattan this morning. So ask."

"You want to get some coffee?"

"Ask here," Moshe Kagan made a large circle with his finger. "My office. Never any waiting." The old man watched a boy, maybe thirteen, counting a roll of bills, a thick roll, as he walked along the street. "You don't ask *him* any questions?" Kagan turned to the detective.

"It's not a crime to count your money. And nobody's chasing him. Two guys say they saw you and Sylvia in the doorway at Fourth and B. You were yelling at her, banging her in the shoulder."

Kagan sighed. "I was not yelling at her, I was giving her some good trade-union advice. Always get paid for what you do. And I wasn't banging her in the shoulder. It was a tap, like you give a child so what you're saying will sink in a little."

"What you did with her before that? Is that what you do with a child too?"

"Cossack!" The statue stared straight ahead.

"Just doing my job, old man. Blondie, the other one, you sure you never saw her."

There was no word from the statue.

"After all I've heard about you from Noah," Dickerson said, "I'm surprised you wouldn't want to help us out. Whoever did this is likely to do it again."

"You want to talk to me," Moishe Kagan said stiffly, "talk to my lawyer. Jason Mendelssohn."

Dickerson's eyebrows went up. "How'd you get to him?"

"You're impressed, huh?" the old man smiled nastily. "How I got to him was your partner. He said to go to him. Why, he didn't tell you?"

"Oh yeah, of course. Slipped my mind."

"So, that's all," the statue announced.

Dickerson nodded, and strode away.

Moishe Kagan took a red bandanna from his back pocket, blew his nose with it, found a clean part, and wiped his eyes.

A sweet little girl, that Sylvia. I would have gone back to her. Brought her a couple of books maybe. Imagine, to cut her in half. Animals don't do such things. We're much worse than animals now. Some God! If there is one, he's like in the movie, with Judy Garland, The Wizard of Oz. *A fake, a frightened fake. It's going to be all over soon. And not only for me, you Cossack!*

25

"No calls!" Jason Mendelssohn, the next morning, stuck his head out of his office and roared at his secretary as he closed the door on her.

"Asshole," the large, elderly black woman said amiably as she put a sheet of paper in the typewriter.

Inside the surprisingly small office, Moishe Kagan noticed a row of framed official-looking documents on the wall and peered with considerable interest at one of them.

"Sure, it's Harvard," Mendelssohn cackled. "What's the matter, I don't look like Harvard?"

"You look just like your father," Kagan said, *Except*, he said to himself, *Max had two arms.* "Your father," he said, "he must have been proud of you, a Harvard man."

The little train that could put his feet on his desk, and smiled. "Ya want to know when my father was proud of me? The day I got a bigger fee than he ever saw in his whole life. And that was only a couple of years out of law school. It wasn't his fault he didn't make big money. He could have pulled down the biggest fees going, but my father took the high ground. It wasn't in him to go the other way. If he did what I do, he'd have puked his life away. Does that make him a better man than me? Sure, it does." Mendelssohn laughed. "That's what he always told me, and I always told him he was right. He was a better man. But always, my father told everybody what I made. The man could have had a worse son."

Mendelssohn put his feet down and leaned forward. "I assume Noah told you that for you, there's no fee. This will be my pleasure. For you and for my father."

"No," the old man said.

"WHAT DO YOU MEAN, 'NO'? Mendelssohn bellowed. "The best fucking criminal lawyer in the country says he's not going to charge you, and you insult him by saying, 'No'? Noah didn't tell me you'd gone senile."

Moishe Kagan smiled. "You get what you pay for."

Mendelssohn nodded. "Okay. I'm not going to argue with that as a principle. But that would not be the case with you and me."

"No reduced rate either. Charge me what you charge your regular murderers and gonifs. I want you to taste the money, all the money, all the way. You'll do better for me if you can taste the money."

"Moishe," Mendelssohn scratched an ear, "you can't afford my regular fee."

"How much?"

"I can't tell until I get into it. But you got to figure at least twenty thousand dollars if they're playing games with you and if it's serious, a lot more."

The old man was writing in a small spiral notebook. He looked up. "My son, he's a millionaire-plus on other people's money. When I get a chance, I make him feel good and guilty that he has no other purpose in this world except to make money. So if I need it, he gives me some of his money and he feels less guilty. This much should make Balfour very happy."

Moishe Kagan's eyes fell on Mendelssohn's desk which had only papers on it, no photographs. "You got kids?"

"One," the lawyer said, walking over to the window, which looked out at a wall. "A *luftmensch*. A butterfly."

The old man frowned. "A *fagele*?"

"No, no. Shtupping girls he can do. If he could get a

salary for that, he'd be in a high tax bracket. But there's nothing else he can do that anybody wants. I sent him over to Noah's wife, she's a reporter, you know. She couldn't figure out what to do with him."

"Tell me," Kagan said after honking into his handkerchief, "does anything get him mad?"

"Ahhhhhhh," Mendelssohn made a sound like a creaky door. A door into an empty elevator shaft. "You got it, Moishe. Nothing makes him mad. Nothing. I tell you, there are times when I'd like to ram his head into the wall. I mean, *into* the wall. Unnatural, huh, for a father?"

"Then that makes me unnatural," Kagan said. "I did it once. Not into a wall. I threw Balfour through a glass door. Smartass twelve-year-old telling me that if the bosses couldn't make enough profits because of the union, the workers wouldn't have jobs, so who was the ILG really helping? Nobody."

Mendelssohn chuckled. "How bad was your son hurt?"

"Nothing. He got up, the pieces of glass hanging from him, but not a scratch, not a nick, not a drop. Listen, it took me a long time, I learned they're going to do whatever they're going to do, no matter what you want. The best thing, the very best thing, is not to live through them, you know what I'm talking about? Whatever they do, it's not you. Then you can breathe when you think about them."

"Moishe, I owe you. I'm already breathing better. Okay, listen, I don't want you talking about anything to do with these hookers who got killed. From now on, anybody wants to ask you anything, tell them they're going to have to ask me. And don't talk about it with your friends either."

"Friends?" Kagan took a White Owl cigar out of his back pocket and stripped off what was left of the cellophane. "Everybody I used to know is in the cemetery or in Miami, which is the same thing. Well, in a way of speaking, Noah is a friend. An acquaintance. So I won't talk to him."

"Him you can talk to," Mendelssohn said, "but with *saychel*. Use your head at all times."

Moishe Kagan nodded. "It's the only part of me that's working at all times."

26

Near the evening of that day, the straight-backed black man, his black tie exactly in the center of his white button-down shirt, was intently reading *The Wall Street Journal* as he walked along Avenue C and bumped into a short, thickset Puerto Rican in his late thirties. The Puerto Rican, wearing shapeless brown pants and an undershirt, gave the black man a mighty shove in the chest, shouting, "Why the fuck don't you watch where you're going?"

Mr. Fitzgerald fell on his elbow, and also shouted, though less loudly, in pain. The squat, swarthy man stood over him, fist drawn back and said, "You want some more. Come on! Come on! Get the fuck up!"

Watching from a prudent distance, passersby of all ages and hues waited, with some impatience, for the conclusion of this chance and maybe fatal encounter. They looked for the glint of a knife, the bulge of a gun, something to send them home with a succulent story to share over the evening meal.

In a low, firm, clear voice, Mr. Fitzgerald, speaking from the ground, said to the watchers, "Do not be afraid of those who kill the body but cannot kill the soul; fear him rather who can destroy both body and soul in hell."

The Puerto Rican drew back a step and looked to the crowd, as if for an explanation.

"Do not suppose," Mr. Fitzgerald continued calmly as he

cradled his elbow, "that I have to bring peace to the earth: It is not peace I have come to bring; but a sword."

"What are you, a fucking minister?" the Puerto Rican's voice still boomed, but rather hollowly now. "That don't mean nothing to me. I know all about churches. They promise you everything. For later."

Still on the ground, Mr. Fitzgerald raised his voice: "When an unclean spirit goes out of a man it wanders through waterless country looking for a place to rest, and cannot find one. Then it says, 'I will return to the home I came from.' But on arrival, finding it swept and tidied, it then goes off and collects seven other spirits more evil than itself, and they go in and set up house there, and the man in whom these spirits now dwell is devoured by them. That is what will happen to this evil generation. That," the black man looked at the Puerto Rican, "is what is happening to you at this very moment."

The Puerto Rican, hands jammed in his pockets, wordlessly growling, made as if to kick the black man, but drew his foot back, wheeled around, and moved swiftly down the block. Angel, who had just arrived in time for the benediction, ran to the black man and helped him up.

"Jesus," Angel said, "looks like you sure messed up that guy's head."

The black man smiled. "It was none of my doing. I merely spoke His word."

"You a lay preacher or something?" Angel looked at him warily.

The black man, picking up his *Wall Street Journal* and inspecting his clothes, started to walk off, turned, and said, "I am a messenger."

27

At the same time, twilight time, in Rafferty's, the juke-box was throbbing softly to Erroll Garner's delicately lustful "Misty." Riordan and Claire, bickering at the bar, stopped to listen as a very large bald man in his mid-fifties, motioning for another gin and ginger ale, began to talk to Dennis, the ancient, runty bartender.

Dennis had asked whether the large man was from the neighborhood.

"No," the man said, "I'm from Washington Heights. Down here on a job. I'm a plumber."

"A valuable man," Dennis, offering a smile so that the stranger could see his friendly yellow teeth, wiped a wet spot on the bar with a dirty, wet rag.

"You know what I'd like to know," the stranger said. "I'd like to know if wrong ever makes right. That's what I'd like to know. Is it wrong to do something wrong if it's the only thing to do to a much worse right wrong. You follow me?"

Dennis said he did but clearly did not, for his eyes had fled to the ceiling.

"I follow you, my friend." Riordan, trailed by his long white hair, moved to a stool next to the large man. Claire, stifling a giggle, moved next to Riordan. "You're not asking that out of the air, I think." Riordan motioned to Dennis to set up another drink for the stranger. "You're wrestling with the real thing, I do believe."

The large bald man looked carefully at Riordan. "It's

real all right," he said. "Well, you look like you've been around the block a few times. You too, miss," he nodded in Claire's direction. "No offense."

"None taken," Claire said warmly. "There's not much on any block I haven't seen."

"So," said Riordan, "if you want to tell us, we'd like to hear about it."

"My son, Mike, was killed," the man said. "Murdered. They got the guy. Found him a block away. My son's blood all over him. No one saw it. A fight in the street, but my son's blood was all over *him*."

"Was he trying to rob him?" Riordan asked.

"They knew each other. My son used to go to a bar in the neighborhood. Nothing heavy. A couple of beers after work. And this guy had started hanging out there. So they knew each other, the way you know somebody at a bar. But this happened outside. This guy said Mike came after him from behind, so the only thing he could do was stick his knife into Mike any way he could. But blindsiding a guy wasn't Mike's style. Never. And how come, if it happened like that fucker said, how come he has to go and beat my boy's head in with a sap he has in his pocket after he sticks his knife in him? Self-defense, he says!" the large man banged his fist on the bar.

"Any marks on the guy?" Riordan asked.

"Oh, he's a cute one. Later, he got into a brawl at some bar and got himself good and worked over. All the witnesses there said he didn't throw the first punch and that three guys jumped him. But he threw the first punch with his lousy mouth. Anyway, he got a lot of marks on him there, and who could tell which came from which fight. Pretty damn cute."

"Your theory, not the cops'?" Riordan asked with some admiration.

"Yeah, they didn't buy it. They said he got boozed up

after the fight with my son and didn't know which end was up."

"So what happened to the bastard?" Riordan asked.

"My son was dead and my son had no record. But this guy had a long rap sheet, mostly assaults. He didn't take the stand though, so the jury never knew about that. But even so, here's my son, married, a year-old daughter, holding down a good job, and here's this floating piece of shit. But his goddman fucking lawyer got him a sentence he could do on one toe."

"What'd he get?" Riordan asked.

"Four to eight, manslaughter. Son of a bitch will be out next year in four."

"I'm surprised he got that much," Riordan said, "with all the pansies on the bench now."

"Well, he had a lawyer that ran over the assistant DA. Ran right over him. One of those Hebes, you know."

"Do I ever?" Riordan clapped the big man on the shoulder. "Tell me, do you remember the name of this lawyer."

"Yeah, I remember. You know what I pray? I pray that one night, that bastard will see his own kid lying in his own blood. The guy's name was Mendelssohn. Jason Mendelssohn. Supposed to be the best there is."

"There's some say that," Riordan moved a little closer. "Then there's some say he's crooked."

"My son left a baby, the one-year-old," said the large, balding man. "I got a chance now to give her something. It can't make up for what she lost, but it's something. This guy that murdered my son is in Dannemora. Also in that joint is sort of a friend of mine. He knows the whole story, this friend of mine, and he got word to me that it'd be very easy to break the bastard's arms and legs. That's my friend's business. He breaks the arms and legs of suckers that don't pay what they owe."

"Anyway, if I want it done, he'll do it. For the little girl, he says. A present in honor of her father."

"So?" Dennis was wiping the bar hard.

"Well, if I say go ahead, I'm behaving like the son of a bitch that killed my son. You know what I mean? It's the way it used to be done, in the Old Testament, and like that. But we're supposed to be New Testament," he looked at Riordan. "Different people. Better people, right? So getting the bastard beaten up, when you think about it, what kind of a present is that to the little girl? What will *she* think about it when she grows up? What will she think of me, you know what I mean?"

"Let's just put this on the table," Riordan said, "and look at it the way it is, no more, no less. Did the murderer get punished enough for what he did?"

"The hell he did," the big man said. "What kind of question is that?"

"Therefore," Riordan went on smoothly, "if he is to get any more punishment at all, where will it come from?"

"But is it for me to give him that punishment?"

"Who the hell else?" Riordan stared at him. "The wife can't do it, the little girl can't do it. You are his father. And as for the little girl, I will guarantee you she will dance and sing when she hears the news—whenever she hears the news. The only thing I would suggest—"

Claire looked at Riordan with delicious foreboding.

"—is that you send the word to your friend to do the job so that the king's horses and the king's men can never properly put the bastard together again. You hear what I'm saying? Leave him bent over and twisted, for the rest of his goddamn life."

The large, balding man sighed. "You're right. You got to be right. And you, miss," he turned to Claire, "do you have an opinion?"

Claire sighed. "I can only say what I would do. I would tell your friend that while he's at it, let him tear the prick off the murdering bastard."

"My God!" Riordan, his face boiling, stood up and kissed

Claire on the top of her head. "In my last years, God has sent me an angel. And because of her, they'll not be my last years."

The big man asked how much he owed.

"Nothing at all, sir," Dennis purred. "All I would like to do is shake your hand."

That having been accomplished, Riordan, taking a sip of brandy, asked the visitor, "Do you happen to remember anything about the detectives on the case?"

"Yeah, a black guy, tall, and there was a big guy, white, he had an easy name, but I can't remember it."

"Could it be Green?" Riordan sang the question.

"Yeah, that was it. The black guy was named Sam something."

"Would you join us in a booth for a last round? Mr.—"

"Just call me Doc, everybody else does."

"Well, Doc, tell Dennis what you'd like."

Doc did, and then proceeded to the men's room. "There is more to this," Riordan whispered to Claire, "than he's letting on. Yet."

"What makes you think so?" she delicately put a hand on Riordan's thigh.

"Instinct, my dear. That's how I became a legend in the department, me instinct. And you," he said behind the bar, to Dennis, "put on the television. Put it on so we can be private in the booth when Doc comes back to us."

28

Around the same time, Noah Green was approaching the Second Avenue Delicatessen with anticipation. Fortunately, his wife was not with him. His wife, who never tired of saying, "That place has got to be getting kickbacks from undertakers."

Green was indeed looking forward to the food, by contrast with the goyishe contents of the refrigerator at home. "*Everything* in here is skimmed!" he once yelled to his wife. But he also took great delight in the countermen, the loony diversity of them. Chinese and blacks and Japanese and Poles who probably hid their crucifixes in their wallets and, of course, Jews. Wiseass kids as fresh as the corned beef and their balding, thick, Yiddish-speaking elders, themselves as tart as the pickles. Every single one of them was a postgraduate professional counterman. Fast, with unfailing accuracy of memory and fingers, and the quality of concentration that would have made any of them Grand Prix winners.

It worked! The goddam country worked, at least here. Green beamed at the countermen from the door. *The melting pot had not shut down. Here it was running as smooth as sour cream.*

He saw the newsdealer at a table in back, eased himself in on the other side. Sol ordered matzo ball soup, a pastrami on rye, lean of course, French fries, Dr. Brown's celery tonic, and apple strudel. Green, frowning at the prospect that his son would never know his father, ordered, with leaping heart, the same. Except for the strudel.

"What I have to tell you," Sol said as the waiter moved away.

Green leaned forward.

"What I have to tell you is that late in the afternoon, maybe five, of the day before that girl, the blonde girl, was found in the garbage can, I saw her arguing with a guy. It was in that vacant lot on Ninth Street and B. I was driving by on the way home."

"You recognize the guy?" Green speared a pickle.

Sol sighed. "It was the statue. Moishe. He was very, very angry. He was yelling. I couldn't get all he was saying, except one thing, something my mother used to say all the time. *A finster in di oygen.*"

Green nodded. "Yeah, my mother wished half the neighborhood blind, let alone Hitler. So what happened?"

"That's all I saw. Last I saw, he was still yelling."

"And the girl?"

"Yelling back. Nothing special. 'Motherfucker,' stuff like that."

Green took a large spoonful of matzo ball soup. It was like drinking sunlight. "Was Moishe close to her?"

"Close enough. He could have whacked her, if he'd wanted to."

"He had his hand raised? He had something in his hand?"

"Nah. They were just yelling at each other."

Green put his spoon down. "Why did you wait to tell me, Sol?"

The newsdealer shrugged. "I like the old man. So he barks a little. He's entitled, an active man with nothing to do. Besides, Moishe reminds me of my Uncle Jake, also a porcupine, if you get my drift. I didn't want to get him in any trouble. So he was yelling at her. So? I figured the whore probably started it."

"So why are you telling me about it now?"

"It's been bothering me, that's why. I can't believe Moishe would kill anybody, except maybe a union-buster, but in this life, what can you believe? I thought and I thought, and I figured you guys needed all the pieces you could get."

"I appreciate it, Sol," Green stared at the huge pastrami sandwich. He took out three slices of pastrami as an appetizer. "You mention this to anybody else?"

"Nobody," Sol said. "Not my wife, nobody."

"Okay, you don't have to mention it to anybody. I've got it."

"The black guy, the one who's filling in for Sam, he comes around, I shouldn't mention it?"

"I'll tell him. We'll see where it leads."

"You think it's possible that Moishe would—"

"Is it possible that you would—"

"You're right. Anything's possible. Even you could do it, Noah. But still, the statue, it doesn't fit. On the other hand—"

"Eat your pastrami, or I will."

29

At six-thirty the next morning, a balmy start of a May day, the statue was standing next to a bench in Tompkins Square Park. Across the path, a large black man wearing a long heavy gray coat was asleep on another bench. A dog without a leash bounded up and down the grass; his owner, a slight young woman, eyes closed, was lost in her headphones.

"I'll buy you breakfast," Noah Green said as he sat down heavily on the bench adjacent to the statue.

"I eat breakfast at six o'clock," the old man stared ahead. "Always at six o'clock. A bagel, toasted, Philadelphia cream cheese, tea, no sugar, prune juice. Sixty-something years the same breakfast. So what does that tell me? It tells me that if I had a different kind of breakfast at a different time, I would drop dead. Anyway, you didn't come to buy me breakfast."

Green took out a cigar, glared at it, and broke it in two. "Why the hell didn't you tell me you knew Blondie? That you knew her well enough to have a fucking argument with her? What is it with you? You're acting like you want us to make you a suspect. What the hell kind of game are you playing? And sit down, for Christ's sake."

The statue was still looking in the direction of the Hudson River. "Standing is good for my circulation," he said. "And my breathing." He took out a red-and-white bandanna and honked into it. "You talk about Blondie. I'll tell you what happened. You're a cop and you're a Jew, so do you remember what that anti-Semite, the police commissioner, wrote in—when was it, boychik?"

Green smiled. "1908. Bingham was his name. My grandfather used to talk about it, and the Jewish cops, the old ones, they used to talk about it."

"THE YIDS MAKE UP HALF THE UNDERWORLD OF NEW YORK CITY!" the statue was shouting. The large black man on the opposite bench opened one eye, glowered at the statue, and shut his eye.

"That's what the *fershtunkina* police commissioner said," the old man went on. "Half the gangsters in New York City was what he called Russian Hebrews. Can you imagine? Talk about group libel."

Green took out another cigar. "Do you remember the thief who wrote to the *Forverts*? The one who signed the letter, 'A gonif from the Tombs'?"

The statue frowned. "You're joking me. I don't remember anything like that."

"No, it's for real. I'll show you in a book I have. The gonif wrote that the police commissioner got himself confused because although Jews were arrested more often than goyim, that didn't mean they committed more crimes than goyim. How come? They were arrested more often because Jewish criminals cannot bring themselves to shoot a cop. So, rather than harm another human being, they let themselves get arrested."

The statue was not amused. "That Bingham, he took back what he said, but even though we didn't come anywhere near being half the criminals in New York, we had our share. That goddamn anti-Semite was not making the whole thing up. That's what hurt, that's what kept on hurting.

"You know what my father used to say?" the statue looked at Green. Banging and banging on the table, he used to say, 'There is never an excuse for a Jew to be a criminal!

NEVER! You hear me, Moishe? If you ever commit a crime, you'll be stabbing the whole Jewish people in the heart.' "

Green pulled the statue by his coat. "So what does all this have to do with Blondie?"

"I noticed her when she was around, which was not very often," the statue said, sitting down next to the detective. "How many blondies like her do you see around here? I noticed where she went, into what buildings, and I noticed what she did to pay for what she bought. Sure, it was none of my business. But it's been a long time since I had any business of my own. So I watched. And I kept watching because something about her stayed with me. Like a cold matzo ball. You know, certain people, there's no way they could be Jewish, and yet—

Green nodded.

"And yet, in your bones, in your *kishkes*, you know they're Jewish. So, a week or so before she died, I'm walking by that lot on Ninth Street and Avenue A, and Blondie, she's standing there, like she's waiting for somebody, and I look at her again, and I say, because it's on my mind, 'You are a disgrace to the Jewish people.' "

"Instead of 'hello,' " Green said.

"What, I'm going to dance around it? And she starts cursing me, including in Yiddish, which gave me a jolt, even though it proved what I knew. Why didn't I mind my own fucking business, and who made an *alter kocker* like me the judge of all the Jews? Like that. So, I give it back to her, and more. I told her I hoped her mother was dead so she didn't have to be ashamed before the world that she brought a whore into the world. A junkie whore! Feh!"

"How long did these endearments go on?"

"Who knows? A few minutes, maybe five, maybe ten. She finally picked up some dog shit, can you imagine, a Jewish girl, and threw it at me."

"She get you?"

The statue rubbed his right eye. "Right here." He sniffed his hand.

"What'd you do then?"

"I made a grab for her, and I got her. I was going to spank her. I was going to spank her out in public on behalf of the whole Jewish people. But she gave me such a klop in the stomach with a rock she pulled from who knows where that I couldn't hold her. She spat in my face and she ran away. That's all."

"All?"

"I went looking for her the next night and the night after. I felt bad. That was no way to help her, the way I talked to her. I wanted to try again, a better way. But I never saw her again, until she was in the paper."

"When you saw her in the paper, Moishe," Green looked at the statue, "Why didn't you tell me about this?

"Do I look crazy to you? There was nothing to tell that had anything to do with the murder, but if I said anything, how it would look, hah?"

"Have you told Mendelssohn?"

The statue was on his feet again. "Next time I see him, I'll tell him."

"Tell him today, Moishe. He's got to know everything there is to know."

"Noah, what the hell is this? There's somebody you work with that seriously thinks I'm a killer? What, I've got a new profession?"

"Sometimes in this business, certain things start adding up in a way that makes it very hard to see any other way to go. They may add up wrong, but before that can be proved, someone's in for a lot of *tsuris*. A lot, Moishe."

The statue honked into his bandanna.

"Moishe," Green stood up, "are you sure that's the last time you saw her?"

"What I said, I said. Now I'm getting annoyed. From

now on, you got any questions, go talk to my lawyer. This window is closed."

"Now you've got it right," Green said, waving and walking away.

30

The next day, early in the morning, Green, reading *Down Beat*, shook his head in sadness. "Nearly all the giants are gone," he said to Randall Dickerson at the next desk. "There's nobody coming up out there who could even hold Coleman Hawkins's instrument case. Or Lester Young's. Or Coltrane's. Nobody. Bunch of wimps who studied composition at Yale or someplace like that. But the giants! Who had the *credentials* to give *them* degrees?"

Dickerson, who had been absorbed in the contents of a thin manila folder, looked up and said, "Crime lab says some of the fibers found on both Blondie and Sylvia Robbins were the same. Wool. But an odd combination of dye colors. One color is a sort of muddy purple the lab doesn't have in its reference files. Could be homemade. These fibers don't match any of Sylvia's or Blondie's clothes. So they could come from something worn by whoever."

"Noah," Dickerson looked at Green, "we need to go for a search warrant. That horse blanket the statue always wears. He must have slept in it in steerage. Looks like wool, and who knows what colors are in it. We know he was with Sylvia. We know they had an argument. So what if he didn't do them both? Unless maybe he did have something to do with Blondie. But even if he didn't—"

Green threw *Down Beat* into a wastepaper basket. "Moishe knew her. I don't mean he banged her. But they had a hell of an argument one afternoon, in a lot, about a

93

week before she was killed. Moishe found out she was Jewish, and on behalf of all the Jews who ever lived, he told her off. She was not penitent. In fact, she opened a rotten mouth to him. And he went for her—to give her a spanking. So he says, and I believe him. He would do it to his own daughter if he had one, so why not to any Jewish girl who had gone wrong? Well, she banged him one in the stomach, and that was the end of that. He says he never saw her again."

Dickerson, shaking his head, stood up and went over to where Green was sitting. "How do you know this?" he said softly, too softly.

"Sol. He told me. And Moishe, he confirmed it."

"Noah," Dickerson's voice was even lower and deadlier, "how the fuck would you feel if I kept something like this to myself?"

Green took out a cigar, studied it, and said, "I was going to write it up for the file and show it to you. I just haven't gotten around to it yet. But Randall, it doesn't mean anything. Moishe doesn't go around killing whores because they're Jewish. He yelled at her, that's all."

Dickerson stared at Green. "I want that coat."

"Sure," Green said. "You got a feeling about Moishe, you got to play it out."

"Don't throw me any bones, Noah."

Green stuck the cigar, unlit, in his mouth.

"Got to clue the Captain in," Dickerson said.

In his office, Fortunato Randazzo listened, his gleaming eyes moving from one detective to another.

"The statue held out on you," Randazzo pointed a stubby finger at Green. "If the newsdealer hadn't spilled it, we might never have known about it. So how the hell do you know he didn't hold out on something else? Like where he put the rest of those bodies?"

"What I know is," Green muttered, "it's a waste of time.

Okay, we got to follow through with the crime lab stuff, but Moishe's not a murderer."

"I am surprised at you, Mr. Noah Green," Randazzo was pacing in front of his desk. "I am really surprised at you. All these years a detective and you come on like Miss Goody Two-Shoes." Randazzo went into a mincing falsetto: " 'Oh no! Moishe's not a murderer! No, no, no. I know it in my little bones. Look into those deep brown eyes of his, how could he murder anybody?'

"There is nobody," Randazzo roared, "NO-BOD-Y who is not a murderer in his gut! What do you think the Pope thinks about, he's staring at the ceiling, it's three in the morning, he's thinking about this pain-in-the-ass cardinal who's making his life miserable and who hasn't got the decency to drop dead. You think the Pope doesn't have his hands around that sonofabitch's throat as he's lying there in bed? So why can't an old Jew, who's pretty quick with his hands, want to kill somebody, want to kill very badly. And this is an old Jew, mind you, who is less and less clear day by day what is fantasy and what is real. You think I haven't seen him talking to himself by the hour?

"So," Randazzo pointed at Green, "he knocks her off because she's a disgrace to the Jewish race. He does it in his dreams, only he's not dreaming."

"And Sylvia, why would he knock Sylvia off?" Green asked.

"Maybe he figured he had to punish her because she was disgracing Martin Luther King. Who the hell knows? All I'm saying is he was seen with both of them, he was seen hassling them, he is no stranger to violence from when he working with the union, so where the hell do you get off with 'Moishe's not a murderer'?"

Green looked at the wall. "He is not a murderer."

"I don't like a mind that's closed tight," Randazzo said. "Not in a cop."

"If the evidence is there, I'll change my mind," Green said. "Even a schlemiel does that."

"Touchy, touchy," the Captain smiled coldly. "I never pulled you off a case. But sometimes it makes sense, you know. It makes sense all around. What do you think, Noah?"

"What would you think, Captain, if you got pulled off a case?"

Randazzo nodded. "You got me right between the eyes. Riordan did that to me once. I never forgave that rummy asshole."

"Why'd he pull you off?" Green said.

"None of your fucking business. Because I'm a wop, all right? Okay, go after the warrant."

As they reached the street, Green turned to Dickerson. "I figured you were going to tell him I've been holding out on *you*."

"You told me what you had," Dickerson opened the door of the car. "Nothing more need be said."

31

Toward midnight, the slight, bald man with a pasty face and bright black eyes was dragging a large, alarmingly high-spirited sheepdog toward the curb of a dimly lit street between West End Avenue and Broadway on the Upper West Side.

"Damn you!" Jeremy whispered fiercely. "In the gutter, in the gutter. Even *you* can't shit on the sidewalk."

"Why don't you bust the bitch?" The low, pleasantly resonant voice behind him belonged to a tall black man who was leaning against a small iron fence as if he owned the whole city.

"Ah, John Lewis, right on time. I can't bust the bitch because it's Mulvaney's, that's why. It came to me, a dog would be a cover for a meet, who could be talking about anything serious with a damn mutt in the middle? So I borrowed this dog from the Chief, but this dog is a retard, and he's too big to be a retard. You got anything?"

"Not really," Randall Dickerson said. "He got the old man, the statue, a lawyer."

"How'd you find out? Stop that!" Jeremy yanked hard at the dog who cheerfully pulled him farther into the street until Dickerson grabbed the leash and brought the dog back to the gutter.

"The old man told me. He said Noah told him he needed a lawyer, or he might need one pretty soon."

"The lawyer's name?"

"Jason Mendelssohn, score one for you. But I found out Mendelssohn's father was the lawyer for the union the old man worked for, so it figures."

Jeremy snarled at the dog, who had urinated in the middle of the sidewalk and then jumped on him and licked his cheek. You ever tell a potential defendant to get himself a lawyer?"

"Yeah," Dickerson said, "when I wanted to scare the shit out of him and shake loose some leads. I mean, when I knew it wasn't him, but *he* thought he might be a suspect. But otherwise, no."

"How's he going to be able to pay Mendelssohn?" Jeremy asked, bending down to pick up a mound of dog shit with the sports sections of *The Times*. "The Chief never told me his dog has diarrhea."

"His son. Big-time business manager. Plenty of bread."

"Part of an ongoing business relationship between Green and Mendelssohn. A steerer. Steerers get paid. Now what other services does Green perform? Got a whiff of anything?

Dickerson patted the dog, who was on his hind feet, licking the detective's nose. "The old man was saying he'd never seen this Blondie, then it turns out a newsdealer guy, saw him having a yelling match with her about a week before she was killed. The guy tells Green, Green gets the statue to admit it happened, but Green takes his sweet time telling me."

"Why did he say it took him that long?"

"Didn't get around to it. Besides, Green says, no way the old man can be a killer."

"Do you know if Green told Mendelssohn about that argument?"

"No, I don't know."

"Bet you he did. Goddamn stupid dog. Will you look at where he just dropped another load of shit? You figure I can ever use these shoes again?"

32

On the twelfth floor of One Police Plaza, in one of the small interrogation rooms down the hall from Chief Mulvaney's large, airy corner office, sat Jeremy; Jeremiah Riordan, former commander of the First Homicide Squad; and a large, bald man in his middle fifties.

"Let me hear it again, Mr. Rinaldi," Jeremy said. "Slowly."

Rinaldi looked around the room, hoping that somehow he had overlooked a window somewhere. "Hot," he said.

Jeremy smiled. "It's hard to be cool in this place, if you know what I mean. But I do apologize. You're a guest, I mean a real guest, and we should have less confining surroundings for guests. I really must look into that. Now, as you were saying—"

Rinaldi took a dirty white handkerchief from his back pocket, mopped his neck, cheeks, and forehead, blew his nose in it, and put it in back in his pocket. "Hot," he said.

Next to Rinaldi, Riordan, tie and jacket on, smiled at Jeremy through yellow teeth. "It can never get too hot for me, Jeremy, as you may remember."

Jeremy laughed. "Commander Riordan and I were on a stakeout uptown, way uptown," Jeremy said to Rinaldi. "A long time ago, before he was elevated. Being kind of conspicuous because of our pallor, as it were, we couldn't hang around outside where this guy lived. We had to get him in his pad, or wait for him there if he was out gallivanting.

"And man, did he gallivant. We figured eight rapes we could hang on him, most of them women over seventy. He'd rob them and then rape them for dessert.

"Anyway, we get up there at five in the morning. We are in an unmarked car that looks as if it had been vandalized at every red light on the way. Just in case somebody's looking. So we tiptoe up the steps, and he's not home. Well, we got to stay up there.

"Now this was one big strong motherfucker. We had to take him by surprise. Even though there were two of us, we want to keep what teeth we had left and all our other parts. Well, this is one little room with a little closet in it. Bathroom down the hall. We couldn't wait in the room because as soon as he opened the door, he'd see at least one of us, the room was that small. So we had to hide in the closet.

"Unfortunately, whoever the absentee landlord of this black hole was, the son of a bitch gave heat. A hell of a lot of heat. And we couldn't figure out how to turn it off. There was no knob on the radiator. The fucking rapist must have bit it off one night in his dreams. So there we were, in this little closet, soaking up the heat, including our own heat, which included our coats because we couldn't leave them in the room and there was no room to hang them in the closet while we were in there and if we took them downstairs to the car, we'd never see them again but somebody might see us. So there we were, cooked.

"Thank God, the prick perpetrator came in maybe a half hour later. I was dying, I was really dying. But this one"— Jeremy pointed to Riordan—"not a drop, not a trickle of sweat."

"I don't sweat," Riordan said proudly.

"What happened to the rapist?" asked the sweating Rinaldi.

"I wish you hadn't asked that," Jeremy said. "We flung ourselves upon him, neck and back, and he flung us off as if we were dust. And as he did so, he gave out with the biggest, loudest, smelliest fart I've ever been in the foul presence of. I don't know if it was intentional or not, but it certainly left an impression. He took the stairs four at a time, disappearing into the blackness that was so congenial to him and his ways."

"Was he ever caught?" Rinaldi asked.

"It's an active case," Jeremy said.

Riordan cackled. "He means some rat in a storage bin is gnawing on the file. The son of a bitch is probably mayor of a large midwestern city by now." He cackled again.

"Well, Mr. Rinaldi," Jeremy was quickly dismissing a chuckle, "tell me what made you suspicious that the attorney for the man who killed your son was getting some inside information from your side?"

Rinaldi lowered his head, frowned, rubbed his chin, looked up again, past Jeremy, and at the wall. "The detective, Green, he took the wife and me out to lunch one day during the trial. We were talking and the Mrs. says how Mike, all the week before he was killed, was brooding about this guy. She says it took Mike a while to come to a boil, but he was getting there. She says the guy was crowding Mike, needling him, saying he only looked tough but was a marshmallow inside, saying things about Janice, Mike's wife, though he'd never seen her."

"Why would he do that?" Jeremy asked.

"Why does a fish smell like a fish?" Rinaldi said. "That's the way he was. And my wife says, he was such a terrible man, it was no wonder Mike finally said he was going to knock his head off."

"Had you ever mentioned any of this to the prosecutor?" Jeremy said softly.

"No. The Mrs. lost control talking to the detective, Green, that day. We had agreed not to say anything about it. I mean, the bastard killed my son. Everything else was off the point. The Mrs. is still kicking herself for saying anything, but that Green, you know, he's such a nice guy, he listens, he knows how to listen."

Riordan cackled.

"So Green asked me what you just asked me," Rinaldi looked at Jeremy. "And we said, no, we hadn't told the prosecutor. We knew Mike, we knew he was just letting off steam, he wasn't going to *do* anything. We knew him. He was our son."

"What did Green say?" Jeremy leaned forward just a bit.

"He said he'd take care of it," Rinaldi looked at him. "Why wouldn't he? Besides, he was such a nice guy. He said he'd tell the assistant DA. Well, the next day, I'm on the stand telling about Mike, what a good son he was, what a good father he was, and this Mendelssohn starts asking me if there was any bad blood between Mike and this guy. And I said they barely knew each other, how could there be bad blood? And Mendelssohn looks at me with the kind of smile that if we was at a bar, I would have wiped off his face, along with his face. And he doesn't ask me any more questions.

"Then the Mrs. gets on the stand telling about Mike. And when it's Mendelssohn's turn, he asks her did Mike ever talk about this guy, did Mike ever say he didn't like this guy, and that sort of thing. The Mrs., she doesn't lie good. She never has. That's the way she was brought up. So she twists and turns and gets pink in the face and coughs and she ends up telling him pretty much what she told Green at lunch. So that stinking Mendelssohn gets it in the jury's head that I was lying. So they pay no attention to anything I said. But the jury believes the Mrs. because obviously, she's telling the truth. They believe the bad blood ran both ways."

"You think your son did go after him? Not from behind, but maybe surprised him?" Jeremy asked the empty chair next to Rinaldi.

"No," the large man put his chin in his hand. "No, I

actually don't. He just wasn't that kind. Sure, he might have said something, the way he felt, but he wouldn't just start hitting without a word. He certainly wouldn't come up on anybody from behind, that I know as sure as I know my own name. No, it was my Mike who was ambushed."

"I see," Jeremy bent one of his fingers until it cracked. "At any point between the lunch with Detective Green and Mendelssohn's cross-examination of your wife the next day, had you yourself told the prosecutor anything about the bad blood between your son and the killer?"

"No. I figured Green had told him and if the prosecutor had any questions, he'd ask us. It wasn't anything I wanted to bring up myself. But once Mendelssohn started asking about it, I knew something had gone wrong because the prosecutor looked like somebody had punched him in the stomach."

"Did the assistant district attorney say anything to you afterwards," Jeremy asked, "about that information being new to him?"

Rinaldi nodded. "Yeah, first chance he had. So we said, 'You mean the detective didn't tell you?' And he finds Green, who was working somewhere else, and Green says, 'It's in the memo. You weren't in, I left it with your secretary right after I had lunch with the Rinaldis.' The prosecutor said if he'd seen any damn memo, _he_ would have asked that question first so it wouldn't look like we were hiding anything, and he'd have been able to work it out so that we could explain it better."

"How did Detective Green react to that?" Jeremy asked.

"He was pissed off. He said it wasn't his fault if the secretary didn't know how to do her job. The prosecutor said he was going to find out exactly what happened, but we never heard anything more about it."

"The only person on the prosecution's side of the case," Jeremy said slowly, "who knew what your wife let slip at that lunch was Detective Green?"

"The only one," Rinaldi said.

Jeremy turned off the tape recorder. "Thank you very much, Mr. Rinaldi. We may have some further questions for you, and I'd like to talk to your wife."

"Sure," said the large man. "Funny thing, she really took to this Green at the beginning. She said he was so kind, she could hardly believe he was a cop."

"She wasn't the first to hardly believe he was a real cop," Riordan said darkly.

Jeremy looked at Riordan, at the red cheeks, the yellow teeth, and the billowy white hair. "My thanks to you too, sir. The Commander here," he turned to Rinaldi, "is as vigilant as ever. If possible, more so."

Riordan smiled. "My best to Chief Mulvaney. Tell him I am always at his service, day or night."

Jeremy smiled. "Oh, the Chief knows. You have a special place in his heart."

33

Henry Langston Fitzgerald lived on the Bowery, the northern end of the Bowery, near the Public Theater. His apartment, actually a loft, was at the top of a six-story building that was witness, as he said, to a time when workmen were proud of their work and builders gave them materials they were proud to work with. Somewhat over ninety years old, the structure had at various times housed printing firms and a manufacturer of men's hats.

Now entirely residential, the building's occupants included several Cooper Union art students, young marrieds who endured the drunks at the doorstep in return for the bearable rent, and a long since retired political reporter for *The New York Post* who had taken to writing novels and to complaining that he was too readable to be published. ("Nobody has to *interpret* me, that's my curse.")

It was a steep climb to Fitzgerald's chambers. The straight-backed black man moved up and ahead effortlessly, but Angel was compelled to remind himself that he really had to take up some kind of sport. Maybe jogging, like that creepy Arthur. Something. He had to do something.

Fitzgerald looked back at him. "Shameful. Somebody your age wheezing like a pregnant lady. God gave you that body and he's not going to give you another one. That's the trouble with gifts. People don't appreciate them. Now if you'd had to put that body together all by yourself, you wouldn't abuse it the way you do. Here we are."

The door was painted black, and attached to it was a large piece of red construction paper on which was printed, with a black felt pen;

THEN THE EYES OF THE BLIND SHALL BE OPENED,
THE EARS OF THE DEAF UNSEALED,
THEN THE LAME SHALL LEAP LIKE A DEER
AND THE TONGUES OF THE DUMB SING FOR JOY.

"Yes, sir!" Angel said. "That'll be the day."

Fitzgerald scowled at him and opened the door. There was one very large room with a sizeable kitchen at one corner next to a window. The rest—not counting a narrow bed in a sort of attic reached by a short staircase—was the living room.

The walls were white and bare, except for a small crucifix over a light switch and a gigantic colored print of a triangle, inside of which was an eye.

"Do you know what that is?" Fitzgerald asked Angel.

"A triangle with an eye in it."

"You have the soul and imagination of a landlord. That is an equilateral triangle and therefore symbolizes the Trinity. The eye, you donkey, is the all-seeing eye of God."

"Great," Angel said, sitting down on a straight-backed chair, there being no other kind of chair. "So what did you want to see me about?"

"You're a tracker. A pretty good one. After all, it took me a while to realize you were tracking me, so you must be good because I'm paranoid. What do you charge?"

"I only done it for myself up to now," Angel frowned.

"Did it is what you did. So how much?"

"What's the job?"

"I want you to find me a wife. That is, a candidate for that position."

"What do I know about—"

"You move around a lot, you're always watching what's

going on, you're intelligent, you're not a hustler, and you read novels, which means you see beneath the surface."

Angel squinted. "What am I supposed to be looking for?"

"Age: roughly between eighteen and fifty. And she has to be clean. I mean she has to be someone who would be terribly uncomfortable not being clean. What she does for a living does not matter, if she does anything."

"Got to be a Christian though, right?"

"Not at all. I'll take care of that, and of any other education she needs. Also, there are no restrictions as to race, country of origin, politics. But there is one quality she must have. She must be good."

"Huh?"

"Are you telling me that you have never known someone who is good?"

Angel looked up at the ceiling and then across the room into the eye of God. "My grandmother, she was good. You know, even though she's been dead for four years, even now she comes to me sometimes when I'm getting screwed up, and she tells me what to do."

"She comes to you?" Fitzgerald stared at Angel. "She appears before you?"

"Nah," Angel said. "There ain't no ghosts. I mean she comes into my mind."

"How was she good, your grandmother?"

Angel shrugged. "She couldn't do nothing bad, what can I tell you?"

"Then you know what I mean by 'good.' "

Angel suppressed a smile. "You said you don't care what kind of work she's in. What about a hooker? I knew a whore once that couldn't do nothing bad, except what she did to eat, and she didn't think that was bad."

"If she is good, and if she keeps herself clean, I will consider her. Do I have to remind you to whom the risen Christ first appeared?"

Angel frowned. "Oh yeah, Mary Magdalene. So what do I get paid?"

"What do you think is fair?"

Angel thought and thought and screwed up his courage and said, "I'll only be able to put in two or three hours a day. I got school and my mother and other things. So, eight dollars an hour. And expenses."

"What kinds of expenses?"

"Who knows? You can't move a step in this city without expenses. Maybe I'll need a cab to follow her, I don't know. Listen, if I'm honest enough to know what good is, you ought to trust me not to cheat you."

"Get a receipt for each item of expense," Fitzgerald said. "And don't go over seven hours a week. Unless you're really on to something."

"Why do you want to get married?" Angel asked. "I get the idea you've been living alone for a long time."

"Fifty-one years," said Fitzgerald as he rose. "That's long enough."

34

Mendelssohn whistled softly as the waitress left the table.

"Beer," Noah Green said. "I ordered beer. What?"

"How long?" the lawyer asked.

"How long what? For Chrissake, you're some criminal lawyer. Becuse I used to be a *shikker*, I'll always be a *shikker*?"

"You want to tell me what's bothering you? No charge."

"No." Green lit a cigar. "Here," he reached down, picked up a plastic shopping bag, opened it, and put a stack of cassettes on the table. "Air checks, mostly. What you have here is ten unforgettable hours of Kay Kyser's College of Musical Knowledge with Ginny Simms, Ish-Ka-Bibble and a lot of other goyim whose names I forget."

"Terrific! I can't tell you how much I appreciate your taking the time to dig this crap up. The client is going to be very, very happy. What do I owe you?"

"It's *bupkes*, forget it. While I was looking, I found a Billie Holiday I didn't have, so it was more than worth the time."

"Come on," Mendelssohn said, "how much?"

Green waved him away. "Hot," he said, taking off his jacket and putting it on the back of his chair. The pastrami sandwiches had come, along with with cream soda for the lawyer and the beer for the detective. Green picked up the glass, took a small sip, grimaced, and said, "It was the schnapps I really liked, not this stuff. Don't worry, I can do without it."

Finished, Mendelssohn lit a long, thin cigar as Green went off to the men's room. He put the cigar in the ashtray, took five fifty-dollar bills from his wallet, also took out one of his cards, wrote "Something for the baby," found a paper clip in his pants pocket, and put the little package in the breast pocket of Green's jacket.

When Green returned, the two old friends left separate tips, paid their checks at the cashier's desk, and walked uptown together, stopping now and then to check out stereo sets, leather goods, and diverse gadgets in the store windows.

Back at Gudaitis's, a cheerful-looking, stocky, round-faced man who had been sitting at a table next to that of Green and Mendelssohn, took out a small notebook, made an entry, and nodded with satisfaction, but then his face clouded. *With what I got for the price of this lunch*, he was thinking, *I should have ordered a lot better. And I should have had that other whiskey sour.*

35

The next morning, the straight-backed black man had come for his papers, as had the pimp who was going to a community college, and all the other regulars. The statue was on the corner, humming *"Kol Nidre."* Quite nicely, the newsdealer thought. With real feeling, but not crying on the floor.

Everything was in order and Sol was about to start in on his bagel with a shmeer and his coffee, still hot in the container, when a round, soft young man astonished him by being there.

"Shel, Shel, where the hell have you been? You all right? You don't look so good. You look terrible. Shel, listen, I'll close the stand and we'll go home."

The young man, shivering in a blue parka, with nothing on his thin blond hair, shook his head. "Listen, Dad, I got no time. I need two hundred. I got to have two hundred. Right now. I can't tell you any more. But you got to believe me. I need it. I need it real bad."

Sol patted the young man on the cheek, said, "Just a second," turned his back, whipped off his belt, opened the zipper on the inside, took out four fifty-dollar bills, threw the belt on the floor of the newstand, and gave the money to his son who rushed away. His father, who desperately wished to yell after him, looked instead to see if anyone was following Shel. No one seemed to be. But who the hell could tell down here?

The more Sol thought about what had happened, the more he felt like throwing up. And before he knew what was happening, he was standing over the curb, throwing up.

"I'll take over the stand," Angel said behind him. "You go home."

"Thank you," Sol whispered, "thank you, no. If I go home, I'll go crazy. She'll want to know why I'm home. What am I supposed to tell her?"

"What happened?"

The newsdealer described the thirty-eight seconds during which he had seen his son.

"You got a picture of him on you I could take for a while?" Angel asked.

Sol nodded, pulled his wallet out of his pants pocket, and handed Angel a snapshot. "But the cops, should I tell the cops?"

"Tell them what, Sol? If he's just a user, they got no time for him. If he's a seller, you could be putting him away for fifteen years minimum. Maybe more."

"At least he'd be alive."

"You got a point. You got another picture?"

"Pictures I have, but how long I'll have the person in the pictures, I don't know."

"Give one to Noah. He'll keep an eye out for your son, and if there has to be a bust, he'll do what he can. I mean, he's got a son now too."

Sol fished out another snapshot. "What should I do now?"

"Stay where you are. Where he knows he can find you."

"Angel, he's my only son."

Angel patted Sol on the shoulder. "He'll be okay." After he'd walked down the street and turned the corner, Angel looked up at the bright sun and said softly, "Sol, you better get one of those little glasses with a candle in it. Just in case."

36

Early that afternoon, a squad car, with Randall Dickerson driving, was moving up Second Avenue to East Twentieth Street and the Crime Laboratory which was crammed into the eighth floor of the Police Academy.

Next to Dickerson was Noah Green and growling in the backseat, Fortunato Randazzo. "It's a lot of crap," the Captain was observing. "One good snitch is worth all the fucking chemists in that place. I can't tell you how many times I've seen smart lawyers, like that sonofabitch Mendelssohn, take a witness from the crime lab and make him eat all that scientific shit."

"I've seen the opposite," said Green, turning around. "I've seen—"

"You've seen, you've seen," Randazzo roared. "Listen, the corpse, he's been run over. And over. No witnesses. Any number of guys would have liked to have run over this asshole. They would have stood in line, their motors running. We pick up a guy. They match some blue chips of paint on the ass of the deceased with the blue paint on this defendant's car. Okay. So in court, the genius from the crime lab swears the chips on the corpse are the same as the paint on the defendant's car. In the pigments of both chips, there's chromium and some kind of copper-based thing. So therefore, the defendant's goose is cooked, right?

"But the defense lawyer, a prick named Mendelssohn, says to the genius from the crime lab, are you telling this jury that there is no doubt whatever that it was *this* car, the defendant's car, that ran over Mr. Russo the asshole? The guy from the crime lab says no, he can't be certain it was this car because there are other cars that also had that paint on them. But there's no doubt that the chips on the corpse's clothes match the paint on the asshole's car.

" 'How many other cars would you say have this specific paint?" Mendelssohn asks, licking his lips as our expert is going down for the third time.

" 'I'd say thousands, the man from the crime lab gurgles as the waters close over him and over the people's case and over the ADA. And you can see this big light going on in the heads of every member of the jury: TILT!"

"Fingerprints," Green said.

"Oh, now you're talking like your head came back on," Randazzo said. "A decent print and you're in business. But the rest of the stuff they cook up over there, we should have that money to put more guys on the street. Guys with eyes."

"Can they see inside pockets?" Green turned around. "Can they look in between the hairs on your head?"

"Hey," Randazzo said to Dickerson, "you see this guy is cracking up and you don't come and tell me? What kind of brother's keeper are you?"

Dickerson, silent, smiled.

"I'll never forget it," Green persisted. "I was up at the crime lab one morning, waiting to find out how much of the stuff I'd bagged a guy with was actually heroin, and I was kibitzing with this lieutenant, Maloney, who is their big guy on trace evidence. You know, glass, fibers, hair, tool marks. And I was sounding a little like you, Captain. 'Don't tell *me* the earth is round!' "

"Watch it," Randazzo said.

"And Maloney looks at me and says, 'Take off your jacket. I'm going to bang it with a stick.' "

"That's just the way I thought they worked," Randazzo said. "Like chimps in a zoo."

"Maloney says," Green went on, "that I have no idea what I'm carrying around with me. So he takes my jacket, whams it with a stick over some kind of lab table, puts a couple of lab guys on what's come off the jacket, and in a while, he shows me, through a microscope, chips of rust and paint, little pieces of glass, dust, soil particles, debris, bits of tobacco, and some marijuana that was in the air somewhere."

"Uh huh," Randazzo said.

"And they look in my hair and they find different kinds of dust and chemical traces. With some of the stuff in my jacket and in my hair, you could pretty well tell where I'd been over the last few days. You pick up different things down on Canal Street than on Park Avenue, you understand?"

Randazzo snorted as they pulled up to the Police Academy, "You and two million other suspects."

Upstairs they were shown into the cramped office of Dr. Victor Bluestone, the tall, thin, reserved director of the crime lab. Glancing at a file folder in front of him, Bluestone said, "The match is a good one. Some of the fibers from the dead women were wool, and each of those has traces of eight dye colors. The problem is, we don't have anything in our references files to check those dyes against. I've never seen anything quite like them before. That coat did not come off a rack. It's handmade. The weaving, the cutting, the dyeing, everything."

Bluestone was talking to Green, much to Randazzo's annoyance. "What makes it more interesting," the crime lab director went on, "is that the dyes are originals. They were done at home, somebody's home."

"But other coats could have been made in the same place?" Dickerson asked.

"Of course," Bluestone said. "But if the others were entirely handmade like this one, it's not likely there'd be any great quantity of them."

For the first time, Randazzo looked interested. "A defense lawyer gets you on the stand," he barked at Bluestone, "and says to you, 'How many coats like this do you think there are around?' What would you say?"

"I would say," Bluestone's voice was clear and firm, "that in all my time in this kind of work, this is the first I've seen. And I would say it was very unlikely there were many others.' "

"And the lawyer says, 'On what do you base that *guess*?' "

"I have directed this lab, with the biggest volume of any city in the country, for fifteen years. If I've only seen one coat and one set of dyes like this in fifteen years, I repeat that it is highly unlikely there are many others."

"Well done," Randazzo said. "Well," he turned to Green, "your buddy was up close to both of them. We got eyewitnesses that he was wearing something that looked a lot like this coat, this coat you picked up from his place. With a warrant. Bring him in."

"It's a funny thing," Green said. "Moishe didn't give us a hard time. He didn't call Mendelssohn. He just gave us the coat, and didn't say a word."

"Sure, it was all over," Randazzo said. "Hey," he turned to Bluestone. "In those dyes, is any of them blue?"

"Yes, why?"

"Nothing." Randazzo moved toward the door. "It's a color that makes trouble, that's all."

Outside, the Captain said to Green, "I'm sending Oliver and Ferruzzi to pick up the old man."

Green flushed. "You afraid I'll let him slip out the back door?"

"I'm afraid I have too soft a heart, you schmuck!" Randazzo said, as he slammed into the backseat.

37

On their way back to the precinct house, Green saw a coat in the window of a church thrift shop on St. Mark's Place. It looked like a twin of the statue's. He said nothing to Randazzo and Dickerson, and a few minutes after they were back on the second floor, Green left, telling Dickerson he had a lead on another of their cases.

When he walked into the thrift shop, Green realized, it had been a long time since he'd had his eyes checked. The wool was thinner, and probably not all wool anyway. The colors were thinner too, and the mix was different. And the coat, he finally saw, came from Taiwan. Nothing in Taiwan was ever handmade.

Remembering a couple of other storefronts in the neighborhood which featured clothes that were way out of style or had never been in style in any place at any time, Green walked toward Second Avenue. A small mutt, just recently a puppy, was sniffing and whining, mostly whining, at a large garbage can that had a most unpleasant smell coming from it. Recognizing the smell, Green turned away and lit a cigar in self-defense. The lid to the can was loose, and Green dislodged it with a light kick to the can itself.

Inside was the young man in the snapshot Sol Weinstein had given him. Sheldon Weinstein. He seemed to be sleeping, a very peaceful sleep in which he was not aware that half of him—from below the belly button—had been neatly removed. He was wearing a faded red T-shirt which announced, in white letters, I ♥ NEW YORK.

After calling Randazzo and the crime scene unit, Green waited by the corpse.

"Schmuck!" Green said to the blond head wearing a disconnected necklace of coffee grinds. "You son of a bitch. "You're about to kill your father too."

An angular, middle-aged woman, a cigarette almost burned out on her lower lip, came down the stairs of a brownstone, saw the head, looked at Green, and walked on.

"Hey," Green said, "you ever see this man before?"

"I don't want no trouble. Whatever there was between you two fellas, let it stay between you two fellas. I never saw a thing. Have a nice day."

Randazzo's car roared up, with Randall Dickerson driving.

"Yuck!" said the Captain. "You know," he said to Green, "if Sanitation had come by before you did, this would have gone right into the mixer. They never see anything, and we'd never know about it. For once, we get some luck."

Randazzo peered at the top half of the young man. "How the hell do you figure this? Maybe he was a male whore? That would connect with the others. Maybe. I don't suppose you know who he is?"

"You know the father," Green said. "Sol, the guy who has the newsstand on St. Mark's Place."

"Oh my God." Randazzo took out his handkerchief and blew his nose. "The only son."

"Two daughters."

"Tell it to Bella Abzug. The only son. Oh my God. Tell me, the statue have some kind of beef with this kid too?"

Green stiffened. "Did you ever hear of the presumption of innocence, Captain?"

"You don't read the papers. The Supreme Court repealed it, thank God. So I asked you a question. Did the old man know this kid?"

"Not so far as I know," Green said.

"Well, that's another thing he and I will have to talk about." Randazzo climbed into the car and drove off. Dickerson, who had stayed behind, asked Green, "Why does he cut them in half?"

"Maybe to make it look like a nut did it. Or maybe there's a new cult we don't know about. Or maybe he designs ashtrays. Shit. I better tell Sol."

"I'll knock on the doors," Dickerson said. "But they probably dumped him from blocks away. Still, one never knows, do one?"

Two boys, about eight, were coming down the street.

"Cross over!" Green yelled at them, pointed to the other side of the street.

The boys giggled and raced down to see what they weren't supposed to see.

They stared, and then giggled again. "What do we get if we find the rest of him?" one of them said to Green.

"New assholes," Green said, "to replace the ones I'm about to kick in."

Laughing, the boys ran down the street.

"What do you suppose it would take to really frighten them?" Green asked.

"I don't think I want to find out," his partner said.

38

Angel, hearing of the murder of the soft young man, ran to the newsstand to offer to take care of it for Sol. But the owner was already gone, and the stand was closed down. Only the big detective with the mournful face was there.

"He taking it bad?" Angel said, just to say something.

"Sol says *he* killed the boy," Green murmured. "Didn't pay enough attention to him. Didn't try hard enough to help him, to find out what kind of help he needed. Did you ever find out if he was doing anything down here besides scoring?"

"He was doing good," Angel said. "He got moved into one of the operations four or five months ago. Smart kid, good with figures, good enough so they were even paying him actual money, along with the stuff he needed to put himself together every day. Then, two weeks ago, they cut him off. From everything. He's been running around like a rat that can't find his hole ever since."

"Why didn't you tell me about any of this?" Green's voice was low and cold.

"Once I found out he was that inside," Angel looked at him calmly, "I didn't want a couple of bullets in my head. I didn't tell you, I didn't tell Sol. These are very serious people, Noah. I couldn't take a chance. Something happens to me, my mother goes in the garbage can, you understand? And to tell you the truth, aside from my mother, I don't

want to die for some junkie. These people, Noah, they'd kill
their own kids, just on suspicion, you know. They have."

"So why are you telling me now?"

"Dead makes it different. He fucked them up some way,
and when they do this to someone they think fucked them
up, they want people to know. It's in the street now."

Green moved close enough to Angel so that the teenager
backed away. "This is the third one. I don't want any more.
I want to know whom you heard this from before it got on
the street."

Angel shook his head. "You want to find me in a garbage
can, is that what you want? Listen, I just hang out. I hang
out with lots of different kinds of people. That's the only
way to learn. You now that about me. You've known that all
along. I tell you what's in the wind, but not everything. You
know that. You push me on this, I got to say no. And
because this means a lot to you, when I say no, you're gonna
put me on the bad pages in your book, that's the way you're
gonna see me, so I won't be seeing you anymore."

"There are no free rides, kid," Noah blocked Angel's
way. "Sooner or later, the conductor sticks out his hand."

Angel closed his face. "I'm not a snitch, and I never said I
was. I told you news, but I never fingered anybody."

"New rules, Angel. Murder makes new rules."

"Got nothing to do with me. I'm not playing the game
anymore." Angel walked off fast, then broke into a run.

A crisp young black woman walked up to the closed
newsstand, shook her head in exasperation, and said, "What
is it, another one of their holidays? Now I got to go three
blocks out of my way."

"His son was killed," Green said tonelessly.

"Oh my. Oh my." The woman looked at Green. "How
did it happen?"

"That's what we're trying to find out."

"Oh," she looked Green up and down. "You're a cop.

Seeing as someone white got killed, I guess you'll find out who did it."

Green flicked his cigar into the gutter and walked away.

"Well, you better," she called after him, "because his father's a nice man. A whole lot nicer than you."

Green wanted to tell the statue what had happened, and he started to look for him. But then he decided to head back to the precinct house. Walking up the stairs, he saw Captain Randazzo coming down.

"How's Sol?" Randazzo asked.

"He said the soul has gone out of his body. And that's just the way he looks."

"Sol's not the only one lost his soul today," Randazzo put a hand on Green's shoulder. "I was just coming to tell you. Moishe's dead."

Green, wanting to sit down, leaned against the wall. "Carved up? Like the other ones?"

"Nah. Heart attack. When Oliver and Ferruzzi got there to pick him up, they couldn't get in. They went through the window, and he was lying there, up against the door. He was on the way out."

"They probably gave him the heart attack," Green said, his mouth sour. "Poor bastard, if we hadn't been leaning on him—"

"I think maybe you need a rest, Noah. You're forgetting the most important thing in this business. You never get personal with a suspect. Either way, friend or enemy. You got to be beyond that. I never saw you forget that before."

"I don't need a rest," Green said.

"I'm taking you off the case."

"Moishe's dead, for Christ's sake."

"He died after the boy. He could have done it. He's still a suspect. You're the guy who keeps pushing the crime lab. Well, they found something. You don't like what they found. Another suspect, you would have liked what they found. Take some time off, Noah. Enjoy the new baby."

"Is that an order or a suggestion?"

"At the moment, a suggestion."

Green shook his head. "I'm no good if I'm not working. No good to the baby, no good to Shannon. Where's Moishe?"

"Mendelssohn," the Captain popped some hard candies into his mouth. "He took care of that. I forget the name of the undertaker."

"I know the name," Green said. "Frank Campbell's. He'll be leaving with the swells. Just what he didn't want."

Randazzo frowned. "Campbell's? That doesn't sound Jewish."

"You got a point," the detective said.

39

He was still a statue, but too vague. Of all the corpses he had seen, this was the most unreal.

Moishe Kagan, in a dark blue, double-breasted suit that Green had never seen on him before, a white shirt, and a maroon tie, had what looked like a smile playing around his candy lips. "The last *greps*," Green mumbled.

Behind him, the stifled laughter of Jason Mendelssohn, who had overheard.

"He looks," the lawyer whispered, "as if he just couldn't stand any more contentment."

"It's obscene," Green muttered.

"Let me," Mendelssohn elbowed Green past the coffin and bent over, as if to take a lingering last look at Moishe, while he slipped a small blue book into the pants pocket of the deceased.

"His union book?" Green smiled.

"The very thing. *Now* there's some Moishe in the coffin."

Most of those in attendance were old, retired members of the International Ladies Garment Workers Union, although a couple of the deceased's younger colleagues, in their late fifties and still organizing, had also come. And there was Balfour, Moishe's son, who looked like Abba Eban and but for his New York City twang might actually have been Abba Eban. Balfour's wife, a redhead, reminded Green of an old Stella Brooks jazz song, "I'm a Little Piece of Leather." Their two teenage sons were politely blank-faced, even when they were viciously digging into each other with their elbows.

"They don't make them like Pop anymore," Balfour Kagan said to Green and Mendelssohn.

"Yep," Mendelssohn said, looking straight at the younger Kagan. "They broke the mold when they made your pop."

"You can say that again," Balfour Kagan said. "Tell me, fellows, what was this, uh, trouble my father was in at the end?"

"He was in no trouble," Green said. "There was a misunderstanding on the part of some of my colleagues."

"Which we still have to put a period to." Mendelssohn took Moishe's son by the elbow. "But you'll be hearing from me on that. Don't worry about a thing."

"You mean," the younger Kagan looked worried, "your services are still required?"

"Just to wrap things up. You don't want any loose ends lying around."

"Oh no," Kagan sighed. "Oh, I wanted to ask you about this," he took an envelope from his inside breast pocket. "Someone left this for me at my hotel."

In the envelope was a check for five thousand dollars from the Lower East Side Family Protection Society, and a letter saying that the donors hoped the money would be used to commemorate, in some way, the departed, longtime cherished member of the community. Perhaps some trees might be planted or some books on labor history bought for the community center. But it was entirely up to the estate.

"You see," Balfour Kagan pointed at the letter, "it's signed by a Robert Mendez. You know him?"

"An errand boy," Green said. "This so-called Lower East Side Family Protection Society is not kosher. Not by me. It's got to be some kind of front. We haven't cracked it yet, but I figure it launders money through some of its donations. It doesn't smell right is what I'm telling you."

"Noah," Mendelssohn said in a tone of mild rebuke, "this is less than hearsay. It's smoke. Is that fair?"

Green looked at him. "You their lawyer?"

"I've represented the society in a couple of small matters," Mendelssohn said.

"That really makes them kosher, right? Listen," Green turned to Balfour Kagan, "your father would have taken that check back to this Mendez and told him to *shtup* it where the sun don't shine. It's dirty money. You catch things from it."

Balfour Kagan frowned. "I don't see what harm trees and books can do."

"That's right," Mendelssohn said, "it's the benefit to the community that counts. If everybody went through life being a purist about everything, nothing good would ever get done."

Green looked back at the corpse. "Moishe's dead, all right. If this didn't bring him over the side, nothing will."

40

The baby was asleep in the bedroom, and on the kitchen table, Shannon Leahy Green was sorting through a stack of clippings in preparation for an interview the next morning with the chancellor of the perpetually sinking New York City school system. Softly, she was singing her way through the statistics:

> *Miss Mary Mack, Mack, Mack,*
> *All dressed in black, black, black*
> *With silver buttons, buttons, buttons*
> *All down her back, back, back.*

"What the hell's that?" asked Noah Green, sitting in the living room and watching the street through the bay window.

"A children's clapping song. England long ago." And she went on:

> *She cannot read, read, read*
> *She cannot write, write, write*
> *But she can smoke, smoke, smoke*
> *Her father's pipe, pipe, pipe.*
> *She asked her mother, mother, mother*
> *For fifty pence, pence, pence*
> *To see the elephant, elephant, elephant.*

"Put on another RECORD, FOR GOD'S SAKE," her husband bellowed.

> _Climb over the fence, fence, fence_
> _He climbed up so high, high, high_
> _He touched the sky, sky, sky_
> _And he never came back, back, back_
> _Till the Fourth of July, July, July._

"JE-SUS CHRIST!" Green roared.

> _She went upstairs, stairs, stairs_
> _And bumped her head_
> _And now she's DEAD_

"Enough, damn it!" Green thumped into the room and, banging his fist on the table, jarred the clippings into nearly total disarray.

"You!" His wife put her hands on her hips. "There is something wrong with you. I was just teasing, and now you've destroyed an hour's work. God, I've seen you edgy, but not like this."

Green sat down at the table. "I'm sorry about the clips." He bent down to pick them up, but Shannon waved him away.

"You'll mess them up worse," she said.

Green took a deep breath and let out the air. "I think I'm being tailed. But I can't figure out who or why."

"Get some of the guys to check it out."

"That's stupid," he snapped. "If it turns out to be nothing, it's going to look like it's time for me to retire. And if I can't handle it myself, then maybe it is time for me to retire."

"Why do you think you're being tailed?" she kissed the top of his head.

"Because I feel I am. And I feel it's from the inside. I've

heard guys, guys with a lot of years, talk about having that feeling. And they've always been right. Of course, they've always had damn good reason to be afraid."

"You mean Internal Affairs?" she said.

"Yeah. But I got no reason to be afraid. So what are they after me for?"

"Could be a cockamamie complaint they figure they have to follow through on?"

Green took a beer out of the refrigerator. "Could be. Could be somebody's setting me up. But who? And it could be that I'm imagining the whole thing. What do they say teachers get? Burnt out? We got more of that than they do. But I never thought it would be me."

She stood in front of Green, lifted his head, and looked into his eyes. "It's not you. If I thought you were even beginning to be burnt out, I'd tell you. But you're not. It's only if you quit that you'll be a basket case."

Green, his hands on her waist, nodded. "Yeah. What the hell am I a detective for if I can't get this thing figured out?"

41

The next morning, Fortunato Randazzo, a steaming cup of coffee and three small, plump sausages at his side, was about to look at the funnies, as he called them, in *The Daily News* when Noah Green, knocking at the same time as he came through the door, said hoarsely, "I want to know what's going on."

The detective, Randazzo noticed, had not shaved with as much care as usual this morning. And his shirt, if Randazzo was not mistaken, was the same one he had worn yesterday.

"Glad to hear it," the Captain debated as to whether Green should be offered a sausage. The Captain decided it would not be good for Green. He, on the other hand, being Italian, had built up immunities.

"Come on," Green had not sat down, "you know what I mean."

"We could save a lot of time," Randazzo said, "if you tell me what you mean."

"Internal Affairs. They're running something on me, right?"

Randazzo laughed. "You know better than that. I'd be the last one to know. They don't tell the commanding officer because if they're right and there's a bad apple, he's responsible for not knowing the guy was a bad apple and for not knowing what he was doing. Oh, once in a great while they let you know what's going on if they need a certain kind of cover for their people, but almost never. They make their own cover. They're like ghosts, the bastards, you never know they're there, but if you believe in them, they're there all right. And we all believe in them, don't we? Why do you think they're interested in you? And sit down, for Christ's sake. I'm not the enemy."

Green sat on the edge of a chair in front of Randazzo's desk. "I feel it. It's nothing I've done, I know that. But I feel I'm being tailed, and by another cop. You ever had that feeling?"

Randazzo wolfed a sausage. "Yeah, a few times. But nothing ever happened. So it could have been them, and it couldn't have been them. Fucking secret police. If they come up dry, they don't tell you they were looking."

"Could be some nut complaint they're just checking out," Green took out a cigar.

"Sure. And it could be all in your head. Like I told you, you could use a few days off."

Green got up. "I can't ask you to let me know if they ask you anything because if they ask you anything, there's no way you can let me know."

Randazzo sighed. "Noah, if they asked about my mother, and she asked me if they asked about her, even as I was kissing her, I'd be lying to her. Look, I can't tell you to get it out of your mind, any more than I could tell myself if it was me, and for all I know, they're after me too if they're after you. All I can tell you is what you know. If it's them, you'll never know until they want you to know. And if you're lucky, you'll never know nothing."

"You're talking like they're magic, invisible, not human."

"I agree with all those words," Randazzo said.

"Not me. I don't sit still so somebody can keep torturing me." And he left, in a hurry.

42

Wilfred Mulvaney had taken a nice nap after dinner. In the music room, the alarm woke him at eleven-thirty. He poured himself an Armagnac, put on his shoes and a seersucker jacket, called upstairs, "Don't lock me out, Mary Lou," and opened the front door.

"How long will you be, dearest?" The buttery soprano floated down the stairs.

"I'll be home for Christmas," he sang, and rushed through the humid air to his car, his unofficial car, a red Jaguar of the best vintage.

Thirty minutes later, he walked into the rectory of an unimposing Catholic church in the Bronx, shook hands warmly with the priest, a short, spry Italian of advanced years, and thanked him for the use of his quarters.

"Not at all," said the priest. "You ever run out of cell space, you can lock up a couple of yeggs here anytime you want. We'll turn them around. We'll turn them inside out. We've done it before. Your man's in there," the priest pointed to a room at the back.

The man Mulvaney had come to see was a woman. Tell, reed-thin, with short black hair and the face of a boxer who had not retired quite soon enough, she wore a cheap blue men's suit, a white shirt, and a green tie. When Mulvaney came into the room, she dragged on her cigarette, flicked it into the fireplace, and smiled at him with what was left of her front teeth.

"You brought it all?" she said in a voice made of thick smoke.

"First the song, my dear. Of course I brought it all. But first, like the man says on television, you must earn it. The old-fashioned way."

"The old-fashioned way, you'd be going up my ass, which you'd like to do right now."

Mulvaney sighed in deprivation, patted her ass which could barely be found, and crooned, "Ah, my girl, the pleasures those in high office must deny themselves. These days anyway. Now—"

She lit another cigarette and lowered her voice. "The three of them, all three of them that got killed, were snitches." She looked at the Chief with a conspiratorial smile.

Mulvaney frowned. "They weren't ours. I know that. Oh! Those fucking bastards!"

He counted seven front teeth left as she smiled more broadly. "And they got no leads," she went on. "No more than you have, I bet. That's why you remembered me, sweetie, right?"

"Tara, will you indulge this rapidly aging party and give me the melody before you do those marvelous variations of yours?"

"Okay, whatever you want. And I mean that sincerely," she chortled. "I've been doing business with them, off and on, for a couple of years. Nothing big, but nothing small either. I get around, I hear things, and though you won't believe it, there are those who want to impress me because I come on like nothing and nobody ever can impress me. Which is the truth. Except for you, sweetness."

"Your business is with DEA?"

"Who the hell else? So, my guy up there, every once in a while, he wants to goose me, he wants more golden eggs, so he tries to make me feel inadequate, can you believe it? How does he do that? By lying to me about how much information some of the star snitches are coming up with. No names, of course. And no specifics, except for a little piece here and a little piece there, and that gives me something to build on in my travels, and I figure out DEA has burrowed into part of an operation, but they don't know who the orders come from ultimately. So they keep the snitches in there waiting for a break, and the snitches come up with some information that leads to some busts, with nobody talking, of course, but a fair amount of merchandise has been lost on those busts and that makes some party or parties unknown very unhappy. So the parties unknown go snitch-hunting."

"What makes you think they got the right snitches?"

She shook her head. "I'm not going to tell you."

"You have no doubts?"

"None." She laughed. "Check it out. Ask your friends at DEA."

"Friends!" Mulvaney very much wanted to spit on the floor, but it was unseemly. "*Your* friends up there, you sure they don't know you and I do business once in a while?"

She smiled through the spaces in her teeth. "How would they know unless you told them? Their records say, and I say, that you pricks have done me dirty every time you could. And that's the truth. I'd never put my ass out for anybody in the NYPD."

"I'll never get there," Mulvaney purred, "but it is a consolation for me to know that you'll be in heaven. How do you know you weren't tailed this night?"

"Because I'm a boy. Why would they tail a boy if they want to tail me?"

"Still, I want you to sleep here, and not leave until it's good and light. And don't drive the old priest wild. Just do the old-fashioned things."

Mulvaney took out a manila envelope from his suit pocket. The woman tore it open and counted four thousand dollars in fifty-dollar bills.

"It makes me feel good all over dealing with an honest cop. How about a fast blow job on the house?"

"My dear," Mulvaney took back the empty envelope and put it in his pocket, "the day will come, as surely as the spring rain, when we shall enrapture each other, and in our honor, the earth will move. But right now, I have an appointment. You will keep in touch? And you understand that's a bit more than a request."

She bowed slightly. "Yessuh, Captain Mick. I go to Riker's Island one more time, all the rest of these teeth gonna fall out and you won't love me no more."

43

Mulvaney left the church and, seeing a phone booth on the corner, broke into a run. He looked at his watch, shrugged, and made the call.

"Galvin? Mulvaney. You alone? Then make yourself alone. I'll be there in twenty minutes. No, it can't wait."

The Chief hung up, ran to his car, and moved fast into Manhattan, going west on Fifty-seventh Street, stopping in front of a large office building. Flashing a badge and a scowl at the night attendant, Mulvaney took an elevator to the nineteenth floor and walked up to a heavy glass door with the neat lettering:

DRUG ENFORCEMENT ADMINISTRATION

He knocked, short and hard. The door was opened by an athletic-looking man in his late forties, his light brown hair short, his eyes blue and noncommittal.

"How were you sure it was me?" Mulvaney said. "It could have been the dark angel of death."

"I could see through the glass darkly that there was only one of you," Kenneth Galvin said. "I didn't have to know who it was. One on one, I've got nothing to worry about." He looked at the gun in his hand before putting it in his shoulder holster. "I don't have Dewar's or Cutty Sark, but the United States Government will gladly offer you some John Begg. Very underappreciated Scotch."

"I am about to tell you," Mulvaney ignored Gavin's waved invitation to seat himself, "that today I am holding a press conference to announce that the New York City Police Department will no longer be part of any Drug Enforcement Task Force involving the Federal Drug Enforcement Administration."

"Gee," Galvin sat down behind the receptionist's desk, "I haven't heard anything from the PC." He poured himself half a cup of John Begg, rose, filled the rest of the cup from the water fountain, and stirred the drink with his finger.

"The Police Commissioner," Mulvaney said, "will take my recommendation."

"Oh that's right," Galvin smiled broadly. "J. Edgar Hoover never died. He went to the NYPD to head up Internal Affairs. Of course the PC will take your recommendation. If you've got nothing on him, you got something on his nephew or his wife's second cousin."

Mulvaney, sitting down next to the receptionist's desk, tried to get his momentum back. "You think Washington will be satisfied when you tell them that? When it's you who's broken an agreement that's been made at the very top. You're going down, Galvin. Maybe they got a place for you as a men's room attendant in the Bogota airport."

Mulvaney rose and stood over Galvin. "You let us go on investigating those murders while you had the key to them, and you had the key from day one. You didn't give a goddamn how many other people got killed who might not have gotten killed if we'd known what you did. The next one could have been a cop."

The blue eyes below registered faint amusement. "The only way it could have been a cop," Galvin said, "was if the cop had been a snitch. All right, listen to me a bit. Wilfred, I don't think I could do as good as you with a force this big. Twenty-four thousand cops to keep honest? What do you got now? So, even if you have an associate in every one of the seventy-three precincts, there'd still be some wormy apples in that big blue barrel.

"Lately, some *very* wormy apples. Wilfred, *we* broke up that cocaine ring the scumbag, Peralta, ran. Motherfucker went around saying he owned that precinct. And he did have two detectives and two patrolmen on his payroll. And they weren't babies. Every fucking one of them had been on the force for at least twelve years. One of them had twenty-four departmental commendations. Makes you want to cry—and bang the bastard's head against the wall. Peralta had stuff worth three, four million one the street every week. And these motherfuckers grease the way for him, give him information from the inside, so his factories never got touched. Until we come along."

Galvin sipped some more John Begg. "And that's not the only one, you know that. Not by a long shot. And you know that too." He handed the bottle to Mulvaney who ignored it.

"So listen a bit more, Wilfred, before you make a horse's ass out of yourself at that press conference. Somebody's knocking off our snitches. *Our* snitches, *capish*? Not yours. If you were me, Wilfred, would you take a chance sharing leads that could be sold to whoever we're after? Not that I know yet exactly whom I'm after, but I know it's not some freak who jerks off cutting people in two. That's what they'd like us to think, and I want them to go on thinking we think that. Gives us an edge. But if we tell the NYPD—nothing personal, I mean that, Wilfred—we could lose that edge because some of your people are AC/DC.

"By the way," Galvin went on, "we didn't know what was going on from day one. We suspected it might be a program against our chosen people, but the blonde, even though she was working with us, ran around with a very unique crowd. I wouldn't have been surprised if one of them had eaten her. I mean with a knife and fork. But when Sylvia got it, the light bulbs went on in our heads. Actually, two light bulbs. You see, she and the blonde were working for us on the inside, but inside two different organizations that we did not believe were connected. Actually, our intelligence was that they were quite nasty competitors. In fact, part of that intelligence came from the Jewish kid who was the third one to get it and who worked for one of those outfits. Disinformation. The creeps who run these operations work like the KGB. None of the three snitches, I should say, ever got above the ground floor, so their killing them was what you might call preventive strikes."

Mulvaney got up, took a paper cup, poured some Scotch in it, but no water, and said, "It won't work, Kenneth. You shut me out of this, who the hell knows how many other things I'll be shut out of?"

"Come on, Wilfred," Galvin said. "You don't want to hear what I'm saying. But let me try again. If it was only you, you'd know everything I know. But if I told you, you'd have to tell the detectives on the case to stop chasing their tails. And you'd have to tell them why. I couldn't risk that."

"That's your judgment," Mulvaney said coldly. "I may give some more thought to whether I want to end this by press conference, but there's no way we can work together anymore. I will not be treated as if I'm some fag in the National Security Council."

Galvin looked up at the Chief. "You're pulling all your people out of the combined task force?"

"Every mother's son. And daughter," Mulvaney said as he started to open the door to the corridor.

Galvin held up his hand to stop him. "Wilfred, on this other thing, now that you know, we really do have to pull together, or we'll lose it. And a lot more. No snitch is going to join up if he figures he'll get carved in two as a reward. Will you keep the press in the dark about the corpses being our people? And will you tell the same to your people down below, filling them full of terror of what you will do to them if they get careless? You do that so well, Wilfred. I— uh— I beg this of you."

"You don't have to," Mulvaney smiled. "What kind of an asshole do you think I am? Never mind. Only a few have to know. We've got too many detectives on the case anyway. After I tell the PC, I'm going to recommend he go with just a few detectives and a captain. Then, if I see anything in the papers that could have come from our people, those fellows will be exceedingly lucky if they get to file retirement papers."

Mulvaney poured more Scotch into his cup, and asked Galvin, "You still have people inside?"

"Some of what we had, which was very small in number, is now on a temporary leave of absence caused by uncontrollable fear. I have reminded them, however, that unlike the piddling time they would get for their sins from the courts of New York, the Federal courts—if these ferrets leave my employ—will give them at least four to five and, if I have anything to do with it, which I do, they could be salted away for ten to fifteen. After all, we did make a deal, fair and square, with these people. They could be doing long time right now without those deals. They fuck up now, they go in. To complete the answer to your question, we do have a couple of dead souls still burrowing away. They are without fear. Quite loony, actually. Do *you* have anyone inside, Wilfred?"

"No," said Mulvaney, picturing the grin of the tall, thin woman in a man's suit.

"Well," Galvin said, "I do appreciate your cooperation, especially after—"

"Think nothing of it," Mulvaney had his hand on the doorknob again. "I'm a forgiving man."

"Everybody knows that, Wilfred. You shame us all."

"If everybody knows that," Mulvaney bowed on the way out, "everybody is full of shit."

44

As Wilfred Mulvaney closed the door of the Drug Enforcement Agency office, Noah Green woke, shivering. He was chilled all the way through, and could not stop shaking. Hugging himself, he left his bed, checking to see if the rattling of this bones had awakened his wife. It had not.

From the closet, Green took a heavy overcoat, put it on, made coffee, drank a cup, and sat at the kitchen table until the shivering stopped.

"You okay?" Shannon said, coming into the kitchen.

"Got the chills," Green said. "I must be coming down with something."

"Stay away from the baby. Want some soup?"

"I want to know what I'm being accused of, God damn it."

"You don't even know you're being accused of anything." She sat down opposite her husband.

"You're a big fucking help." Green pulled up the collar of the overcoat. "If I tell you IAD is after me, they're after me. You know your business, I know mine."

She looked at him, shaking her head. "Noah, you're letting them drive you crazy."

"What the hell am I supposed to do?"

"Go see—what's his name?—Mulvaney."

"Sure," he reached into the overcoat for a packet of cigars. "If they're not ready for you, they don't know you.

'Why, Mr. Green, whatever made you think we were interested in you?' "

"Sure there's nothing you want," his wife said.

"Nothing, thanks." He put out the cigar.

"Well, I'm going back to bed. I got to see the Board of Ed
guy at eight."

"Yeah."

"You got a fever?"

"No."

"Noah, if you haven't done anything, you got nothing to
worry about."

He snorted. "That's what I tell them all. And then they
get sent away. Get some sleep. If I don't leave a note,
everything is yours. Except for the Billie Holiday records.
They're for the baby."

"Very funny." She stared at him.

"Oh come on, if I was going to do it, I wouldn't advertise
it. Listen, where's some paper? And a pen?"

Shannon went into the back room and came back with
some of her newspaper's stationery and a black felt-tip pen.
"Can I ask?" she said.

"I'm going to go all the way back," Green said, "and see
if I can find anything they could be after me for. Something
I did they could have gotten wrong, you know?"

"Then what?"

"Then I'll be ready."

"Yeah."

45

For the rest of the night, when Green slept, he slept at the kitchen table. When he got up for the last time, Shannon had left and the housekeeper was there, looking at him with the particular kind of amusement that comes from an onlooker being privy to signs of a domestic spat.

"I'm coming down with something," Green mumbled, "and I didn't want to give it to Mrs. Green." Why the fuck did he have to explain himself to her? Might as well get in the habit.

At the precinct, upstairs, talking low, Green told Dickerson what he suspected. "You think I'm crazy?"

"You're no more paranoid than it takes to stay alive," Dickerson said. "You could be right."

"Anybody ask you anything that could be from them?"

"About you?"

"Yeah."

Dickerson shook his head.

"And you heard nothing."

"Nothing."

"So what do you think I should do? Go down and see—what's his name?—Mulvaney? Doesn't that make it look like I'm so worried, they got to be right?"

"Depends on how you come in there. You go in looking green, they're going to pump you out. You go in mad as hell—but you got to *really* be mad as hell—they're going to start wondering if maybe they got taken by some tipster. Why aren't you mad as hell, come to think of it?"

"I forgot." Green smiled. "I mean it. They got me going so that last night, I even started trying to figure out how they might *think* they're right. And nothing came up. I'm so clean, I'm embarrassed. God damn it!" Green banged his fist on Dickerson's desk. "Who the hell do they think they are? The Gestapo?"

"Ask them," Dickerson said, taking a bite out of his toasted bagel.

46

That afternoon, at Rafferty's, Jeremiah Riordan and Claire were watching Katharine Hepburn and Spencer Tracy having words.

"Too bony," Riordan looked up from his Gordon's gin. "You'd get in bed with that and in the morning, you'd be black and blue all over. Still, the grandest thing about an uproar like they're having is when the blood is all the way up in you and that's not the only thing that's up, my, what a mighty coming together there is at the clashing climax of the argument. We should argue more, my dear."

"I'm not an arguer," Claire signaled Dennis for another glass of white wine. "I see everybody's side because everybody has a side. Tell me, Jeremiah, why do you hate that Noah Green so? What has he done to you?"

"He blames me, all over the department, for not having risen, for not having succeeded me. He says I got Randazzo in only because Green is a Hebe. That's what he says."

"And is it true?"

"Of course it's true," Riordan shouted, causing Dennis to ask if there was anything wrong with the gin.

"The gin is fine, mind your own business," Riordan growled.

"Then why," Claire put a hand on Riordan's arm, "do you hate him if you're the one who harmed him?"

"Because I didn't finish him off. He's a walking reminder of one of my biggest failures. He has no business being in the department. None of them Hebes do, but him especially. Hebes think only of their own, and you can't have that in the department."

Claire looked at her glass of wine. "But why is it Green you always get to when you talk about Jews? It's as if you see him as more than a Jew. It's as if you see him as the Devil."

"Ah," Riordan bared his yellow teeth in a sharing smile. "Through the centuries, my darling, there have been a few of us who have made a serious study of Darkness. That is, who study Satan and his creatures. Most of us believe that Satan will never be destroyed, only dislocated and then not for long."

"God, you see, insists on maintaining evil in the world so that He will be more desperately appreciated. He's rather vain that way, God is. But Satan, of course, takes advantage of God's vanity by continually striving to prevail. Satan works his plots through the souls he owns, and he can only be kept off-balance by preventing those foul creatures of his from gaining power, wherever they are. Jews are not, of course, Satan's only agents, but all Jews *are* his agents."

"How do you know that?" Claire asked softly.

Dennis had inched close to the end of the bar where the two were talking. "What do you want?" Riordan barked at him. "You've heard all of this."

"I always like hearing it again," the bartender said. "If you'd make a recording of it, I'd go to sleep by it."

Riordan turned to Claire. "How do I know every Jew is possessed by Satan? Have you heard one of them, just one, say he was sorry—not in anguish, just sorry—for his ancestors' having killed Christ? The words could not leave their mouths. Satan would stuff them back in. Oh, there's much more proof. I'll show you some books that are long out of print. The Jews, they owned the publishing houses, you know, so they have stopped the printing of books like these that tell the truth.

"Now at the time of my last difficulties with this Green, I was nearing compulsory retirement, and I knew that if Green took over, he would gradually, they're so clever, bring others of his race forward in my command and that he would push for the promotions of other Hebrews elsewhere in the department. And before you knew it, the police force would be run according to the Talmud, which of course is Satan's book, and which says that neither Christian lives nor Christian property is worth a Jew's spit."

"How did you stop Green from rising?" Claire asked.

"By saying—not writing it down but saying it in only the right places—that he wasn't a team player and that, well, he was prejudiced, deeply prejudiced, against Christians. It was too bad, I said, him being so intelligent, but this, after all, was not the police department of the state of Israel."

"And now you want to destroy him completely?" Claire caught Dennis's eye and pointed to her glass.

"You miss my meaning," Riordan said. "I do not want to destroy him completely. I want to displace him. Get him off the force for good. At his age, he can't land anywhere else where he can do harm, smart though he is. Then I can rest, my dear, and maybe we can go to Atlantic City."

"I don't know this Green," Claire said to her glass of wine, "but I've known some Jews, and they've been like everybody else, good and bad."

"You're too innocent a thing," Riordan leaned over and pecked her on the ear, "to see into Darkness." Watching Dennis go to the front of the bar to attend to a new customer, he whispered to Claire, "Would you like to make me a very happy man?"

She giggled. "Last night, you said I'd already done that."

"Yes, yes indeed," he put his hand on the inside of her thigh. "But this is another thing entirely. I want to know exactly where the Hebrew has his desk now at the Ninth precinct, but I don't want to be the one there asking. I want to ask you to find out for me, and to do one other thing. In a wee second, when people are otherwise distracted—it happens often up there—just leave a note for Green on his desk."

"A note?"

"That's all, my dear. A simple note."

"What will it say?"

"I'll show it to you before I seal the envelope. I would never leave you in the dark. Not alone in the dark. Come, let us celebrate in the dark."

"Celebrate what?"

"Why, as is our custom, the triumph of virtue—and a kick in the balls to the Devil."

47

Late the next morning, Riordan stopped in front of a long, large bar and grill on Sixth Avenue near Forty-third Street. "This one," he said to Claire. "We'll have a beer or two, and then you'll call."

"Why this one?" she looked at the ten-o'clock rummies stuck to the bar, and at the black slab of pastrami being seasoned with cigarette ashes by the chef standing over the grill. The salami, Claire thought, looked just a bit surlier than the chef.

"Why this bar?" Riordan opened the door for Claire. "It's nondescript. Just as, if you'll forgive me, my dear, we are. Nobody'll remember we were here, because we barely were."

They sat down at the end of the bar near the door. "Now," Riordan said, handing her a slip of paper, "you'll call the number there, and you'll ask for Green. Noah Green. If he answers, hang up. If they say he's not there, ask what tour he's on."

"Tour?" Claire looked at him.

"You're right. A civilian wouldn't know the word. Just ask when he'll be on again. And then you'll be there when he's not."

"Go over the hard part slowly," she said.

"Shush," he smiled at her as the bartender came toward them. Smiling at the bartender too, Riordan ordered two Buds.

After the beers were delivered and begun, Riordan continued softly: "All that's left for you to do then is go down to the precinct and ask to see a detective. Any detective. The desk sergeant will ask you why you want to see a detective. You will tell the desk sergeant that it's a very private criminal matter and that he will understand why you can only bear to tell it only to the detective. You will drop a tear or two at that point. Can you do that, my darling?"

"Yes." She sighed. "I shall think of my mother who told me never ever to lie for if I did, God would not want me in his heaven. Ever."

"And your mother never lied?"

"Never. Mother was the most hated person on the block, especially in our family."

"So why would thinking of her bring tears?"

"Because she used to embarrass me so in front of my friends."

"Well," Riordan drank more beer, "be that as it may, since you don't look or talk balmy, someone will bring you upstairs. When you get there, you will tell the detective to whom they bring you that you've just remembered the name of the man you talked to before. Yes, you were there once before. You saw Detective Green. It's him you must see. Now. And the detective will say Green is not there. And you will say, 'When I come back, for it is him I must see, where is it that he sits?' You will also say, 'I was so upset the first time I was here, I don't remember where he sits. Such a kind man he is.' And the detective will point to Green's desk and you will then thank him and curtsy."

"Excuse me, mate," a tall man with filthy blond hair, one purple eye and the other entirely closed and out of business, with blood trickling down his face from somewhere in his matted hair, stood behind them. "I'm from Sydney, mate, new here, and I got terrible taken advantage of. Could you stake me to a whiskey so I could get myself together?"

"Why don't you go downtown to *The New York Post*?"

Riordan said. "It used to be an American paper, but an Aussie owns it now. He'll make you an editor."

"Oh Jeremiah," Claire said, looking in her purse.

"No you don't," Riordan took the purse from her. "Unless you got a gun in there."

"Hey, mate," the newcomer said, turning up a whine. "I'm a human being just like you. Remember Jesus and how he touched the leper and cured him."

Riordan sniffed. "The Jesus I remember is the one who came up to the fig tree, and when He found there was no fruit on it, only barren leaves, Jesus cursed that useless tree, and he said, 'May no one ever eat fruit from you again!' "

"You ought to be ashamed," the down-under whine grew louder, "speaking of Him that way."

"Hey, mac," the bartender, a big, booming lad, pointed at the Australian. "Out!"

"I got money," the visitor rasped. "What's a beer?"

"Twenty dollars," said the bartender who reached under the bar for a billy club, held it lovingly in his hand, and watched the Australian move spiritedly out to the sidewalk.

Claire looked after the Australian. "I think he was crying."

"I should hope so," Riordan said. "Disgracing his country like that. Well, that's what happens when you populate a place with convicts. Now, after you've got a fix on Green's desk, you'll tell the detective who told you where it is that you've changed your mind and you can't wait to talk to Green. You will talk to this kind man.

"This detective will take you to his desk and you will tell him that they have not only not stopped watching you but now they are sending messages to each other through the tiny, tiny transmitters they have placed in your teeth. And they don't mind you hearing those messages on how they plan to drive you crazy because they know that no one on the outside would believe you if you told them.

"At this point," Riordan took a swallow of beer, "the

detective, whoever he is, is trying to figure out the fastest way to get rid of you. But you are quick to say that they have also placed tiny, tiny transmitters in the bottom drawers of every desk of every detective in the precinct in case one of them somehow comes to believe you. They want to know if that happens, because then they'll try to drive that detective crazy too.

"The detective now sees you as a fruitcake, but you look at him with those summer-by-the-sea blue eyes, and you say, 'Sir, I beg of you, open you desk. I know it's in there because I heard them say so inside my teeth. Please, so you'll know I'm not a crazy woman, open the drawer.' And to humor you, he does, and what do you know, no transmitter. You will say, 'Just one more bottom desk drawer. They saw me coming to you so they whisked the transmitter away from your desk. But if I pick a desk at random, it'll *be* there! But if I'm wrong this time, I'll leave. I'll leave right away.' Well, that's the best news he's heard all month, so he says, 'Okay, which desk?' And you point to Green's, and you rush over there, and while your back is to him, you slide the letter under the ashtray or something on top and then you open the bottom drawer and damn, the clever little friends have outsmarted you again. So, with a nice, warm, desperate smile, you leave."

"I know this must be a dumb question," Claire said, "but couldn't you have *mailed* him the letter?"

"Anyone can mail a letter, my dear," Riordan grinned. "But not anyone can be so familiar with where a detective works that he can be his own mailman, walking about the place as if he belongs there. And why would he not belong there, if he can do that?"

"Tell me again what the letter I'll be delivering says."

"Very simple, very clear. It says: 'Green, Internal Affairs is on to you.' "

"He'll be very upset," Claire said. "Especially getting the letter that way."

"Oh he'll be banging into himself forty different ways. He'll drive himself crazy. He'll be biting his toes before he's done."

"And then you'll be at peace, Jeremiah?"

"Except between the covers," he touched her thigh. "God is good, Claire, he settles each and every account when it's time."

48

Green wasn't due in until four that day, but he started looking for Angel early in the morning. The door of the apartment on Avenue B and Second Street was open, Angel's mother snoring on the kitchen floor. But there was no sign of Angel. Green went through the parks and playgrounds, going as far west as Washington Square. He went back east, exploring the streets and avenues. He looked in at The Strand bookstore on Broadway, the bookstore on St. Mark's Place, and the bars. The kid liked to read in bars. At Sol's newsstand, still locked up, Green stayed a while, figuring Angel might come by out of habit.

At the edge of the Bowery, near the stairs going down into the Astor Place subway, Green saw a familiar face, what was left of it. A black patch with spots of what looked like peanut butter covered the right eye of the small man in his early thirties with rust hair and brown pitted skin. He was wearing a light-blue T-shirt that announced, I'M NOT EASY BUT WE CAN DISCUSS IT, black pants that looked as if they doubled as pajamas, no socks, and yellow thongs. On an upended wooden crate, covered by a Chinese newspaper, there were rows of sunglasses, sprinkled with some cigarette lighters and wallets.

Green picked up a wallet, examining it closely.

"He's in trouble," the vendor said softly. "They didn't mind him talking to you before. They thought he was like one of them puppies that likes *everybody*. They didn't take him seriously is what I'm saying. They didn't think he knew anything to tell you, and he didn't." His voice rose as a young woman approached, heading for the subway stairs. "Every one of those wallets is handmade, sir, in England."

"Then why doesn't it say England on them?" Green glared at him.

"Because of the educational system there, sir, the class system, you know. The poor blokes couldn't spell it right, which is how it came out Taiwan. You see, if you're a member of the lower classes in England, sir, you never even get taught your ABC's proper. So you do the best you can."

The young woman disappeared down the subway stairs.

"They lost a lot of bread and some very experienced cats because of your snitches," the vendor said as he showed Green another wallet.

"They weren't ours. Ours have come up with *bupkes*. The way I figure it, the feds must've had snitches working in there. Damn feds. They treat us like we're the Russians. But tell me, how the hell did they keep their busts out of the papers?"

The vendor smiled innocently. "Because they didn't tell the Russians?"

"Fuck you."

"Anyway," the vendor continued, "the President should have such security as the other guys got now. They're taking no more chances. That's why they're looking for your boy. Even though they know he knows nothing, they want to be sure. Like you cats say, they want to ask him a few questions."

"You seen him?"

"Not for a couple of days. He has very big ears, that boy. I figure he heard they were looking for him, and he split."

Two rummies of indeterminate age and capacities were coming across the street, in the direction of Green and the vendor.

"Sir, I will personally guarantee that particular wallet

not only against defects in workmanship but against it ever being lifted from you by one of our crooky citizens. You see, it is finger-odor activated. If any other finger but its owner's is placed on this wallet, it will yell, 'A dirty rotten thief has hold of me!' It will yell this in Chinese, of course, because this was indeed made in Taiwan—we are laggard in these matters in the West—but the cry is so blood-chilling that the perpetrator doesn't have to understand the words. He will drop this wallet like a hot knish."

The rummies kept going toward Second Avenue.

"I'll ask around some more," the vendor said. "I'm not optimistic, my friend. I don't think any one of them had a mother. I think they were brought up in schools of piranha. I shouldn't be talking to you myself, but I owe you. Besides, they think I'm not all here, or anywhere."

"They. They. Who the fuck is they?

"Bite your tongue. You want to know what I think, though?"

"Yeah?"

"Up top, way up top, is one hell of a computer."

Green tossed the wallet back, shook his head, and walked east, dreading each row of garbage cans but unable to stop himself from opening each one with a cover on it.

Arthur, running with his customary ease and grace along East Fifth Street, slowed as Green replaced a garbage can cover. "It really is a shame," said Arthur, gliding slowly, "how you people are underpaid, having to supplement your diet like that."

49

Green came into the station house a ten of four, walking right past the Captain, who was also going upstairs.

"What am I, you don't nod even?" Randazzo barked. "A ray of sunshine, a song, I never expect from you, but I'm entitled to a passing recognition that there is a Fortunato Randazzo on this earth and that whether you wish him well or not, you *see* him. Am I wrong or am I right?"

"My apologies," Green said, "I was thinking."

"You can't see what's around you and think at the same time? Some cop. What's bothering you?"

"I can't find Angel. And I'm not the only one looking for him."

"Who else?"

"Dealers, big dealers. I don't know who they are yet."

"If somebody doesn't drop a dime," Randazzo said in disgust, "nobody knows anything around here."

Green went upstairs, sat down at his desk, took out a cigar, threw the cellophane in the ashtray, saw a letter under the ashtray, opened it, read it, bit his thumb hard, rushed into the Captain's office without knocking, and dropped the letter in front of Randazzo.

"What the hell's going on?" Green, his voice choked, said.

Randazzo read the letter, read it again, looked up at Green, and said, "Why would I know any more than I did the last time we talked about this? First, sit down and calm down or you're going to have a stroke and Shannon will get married again and some other guy is going to be the father of your son. And you know what stepfathers are like. So take a deep breath. Take a cigar. Here, take some sourballs, I got a sausage left from this morning, and you know it could be a joke? Some of your playmates out there have a sense of humor that goes with plastic turds.

"Or," Randazzo handed the apothecary jar to Green who dug in, "it could be some civilian who wants you to sweat. All the time you've put in, you got to have a streetful of enemies. I mean think about it, Noah, get your *Yiddishe kopf* screwed back on. If Internal Affairs is interested in you, why the hell would they let you know? So you could cover your tracks? Makes no sense."

"They could have done it," Green said, "so I'd panic and act like I was guilty of something."

"First of all, it's nice of you to cooperate with them, if that's what they're doing, and second of all, *schmuck*, if you haven't done anything, what the fuck difference does it make if you act, if you look, like you're guilty? Jesus, you're coming apart."

Green, sweating in a new beige summer suit from Orchard Street, at the first sight of which his wife had laughed so hard that the baby started crying, looked at Randazzo and looked out the window. "This surveillance thing is murder. It's creepy. Eyes, ears, you don't know where they are, but they're on you all the time."

"Oh shit," Randazzo said, "you don't even know if you're being surveilled."

"See what I mean?"

Randazzo sighed. "What am I going to tell you? It's no good for you to take time off now. You'll go crazy. But how are you going to work if you can't think of anything but eyes and ears in the woodwork?"

"I know what I'm going to do," Green rose. "I already made up my mind, I should have done it already. I'm going to Mulvaney and straighten out all this crap. I'm going right now."

"You can see the Pope easier without an appointment than Mulvaney. He hates surprises. Call him up."

"Nah. That way he can stiff me. I'm going down. I got to do something."

"Well," Randazzo leaned back, "you got nothing to lose, I guess. Listen, you're going to be down there, bring me back a double order of fried dumplings. You don't have to hurry back. I like them cold."

Randazzo waited a few minutes, got up, closed the door all the way, picked up the phone, announced himself, waited, and said, "Chief? Fortunato. Randazzo! How many Fortunatos you know? Yeah, I can come down tomorrow at nine, but I didn't call to make an appointment. Oh, you were going to call me today. So what's it about? Somebody tipped you to the cathouse we got out in back? Oh, about the murders. Yeah, sure.

"Listen, what I called you about, this thing with Noah Green, how serious is it? What do you mean what thing with what Green? Oh, I get it. What do you mean *should* there be something about Green? No, I never noticed anything funny. Wait a minute though, he's a big worrier, maybe he's got something to worry about. Listen, I'll do a check. You don't want me to. Okay, Chief, see you tomorrow."

Randazzo, frowning, picked his nose. "I'm gonna do it anyway," he said. "The double talk he was giving me, he's got something on Green, all right. Wants me to keep me out of it so I can't cover my ass and when they bust Green, who else takes the fucking fall? His commanding officer is who. They'll send me to Staten Island, back to running a detective squad, if that. Or they'll hint, like with a hammer, that it's time for me to file my retirement papers. Open a trattoria. Or a classy shoe repair place. Put a picture of

Pavarotti in one window and Geraldine Ferraro in the other. The ship of the has-beens.

"Goddamn!" Randazzo walked to the window and looked out at the police cars and the kids playing in the street. "I was getting used to it here, I was building something here, and now it's all over. Goddamn Green. Well, you know, they're right. I should have seen what was going on, whatever the hell it is."

50

Uptown a few hours before, Angel, luxuriating in his anonymity among the crowd at Forty-fifth Street and Fifth Avenue, was thinking, *You live in a little place in upstate New York or wherever, it's all over. They just have to turn the corner, and they got you.*

Still, he looked over his shoulder and was pulled back to the parade as the band came in sight, playing "The Battle Hymn of the Republic." Directly behind the four young men playing snare drums came a cluster of middle-aged men and women walking under a huge cloth sign, WE LOVE OUR CHILDREN, as bystanders cheered, "Yeah, moms and dads!"

They were followed by a sprightly group of elderly men in straw hats with red-white-and-blue hatbands that proclaimed: GAY SENIOR CITIZENS. Behind them were AMERICAN GAY FLORISTS (*In God's Garden Not All Stems Are Straight*).

Angel gaped at the next contingent, four solemn young Catholic priests, in black clerical suits, bearing a placard: THERE CAN BE NO LOVE WITHOUT JUSTICE. But Angel smiled at the merry members of THE GAY EPISCOPAL SOCIETY (*And Lo! The Lord God Saw That It Was Very Good*).

During a lull to let the cars cross the avenue, Angel sneaked another look behind him, saw nothing suspicious, and turned back to see a black baton twirler marking time

by chanting, cocking his head in rhythm, at a beefy, uniformed cop in this thirties a few feet away:

> _"Two, Four, Six, Eight_
> _How Do You Know the Cops Are Straight?"_

Taking a Hershey almond bar out of his back pocket,
Angel munched contentedly as he eyed the Salsa Soul
Sisters, the Dykes of Hoboken, six lesbians in wheelchairs,
followed by LESBIANS IN HEALTH CARE, and, wearing blue open-necked shirts and jeans, marching in neat but
relaxed formation, THE GAY OFFICERS LEAGUE,
NEW YORK CITY POLICE DEPARTMENT.

On-duty police keeping the crowds on the sidewalks reso-
lutely ignored their colleagues on parade, although the
backs of the working cops spoke volumes.

Five men in a jeep, each in black leather, including black
gloves, moved slowly down Fifth Avenue. One of them held
aloft a cloth sign, TOTAL SEXUAL LIBERATION, S/M.
Another, blond and slender, was sitting on the lap of a
stocky, black-haired man with a short, neatly clipped beard.
Next to them, the driver glowered straight ahead. Standing
on the backseat of the jeep, a man in his early twenties wore
chains around his neck, the chains bouncing against his
bare chest.

As the man with the chains turned from one side of Fifth
Avenue to the other, apparently blessing the multitudes,
Angel noticed an opening in his black leather pants which
allowed a partial view of his naked buttocks. When the
young man turned all the way in his direction, removing his
jacket, Angel discovered the man with the chains had lost
his left hand somewhere. Riveted by the stump, Angel
heard a soft voice behind him, "I wouldn't jump to any
conclusions, sweet Angel. On the other hand, I'd hate to see
what's left of that boy if he ever reaches fifty."

Angel ran, right in front of the jeep, as the one-handed

man reached out as if to embrace him. Just before he got to Madison Avenue, Angel looked behind and saw a loping, smiling Arthur. Without breaking stride, Arthur, catching Angel's eye, opened his shirt just long enough for Angel to see a long-bladed knife strapped to his side.

"Shit," Angel muttered, "I bet that fucker's at least six inches long."

From the parade back on Fifth Avenue came the strains of "God Bless America," with Kate Smith's naturally clanging voice so vibrantly amplified that it was as if she had come back from the dead but was so addled by the journey that she couldn't stop shouting.

Angel, knowing that while he was faster in the short, desperate run, his pursuer had more stamina, figured he had only one chance. Find a cop. And coming up Forty-fifth Street from Lexington Avenue came his deliverance—a slight, red-haired policewoman in her early twenties, twirling her billy club with breezy assurance. Angel fell at her feet.

"He's going to kill me," Angel pointed at Arthur, who, however, had already delicately wheeled around and slipped into the lobby of the Roosevelt Hotel.

"Jerk," the slender policewoman snapped at the fallen Angel, "get your filthy hair off my shoes."

"Officer," Angel said as he rose, "you saved my life. When he saw you, he ran away. I'm going to dedicate the rest of my life to you. I would be honored to know your name."

"Get lost, jerk," she said, twisting her perky Italian face into a snarl.

Angel did just that as the cop's snarl turned into horror and disgust, for coming up the street toward her was a lamb who had strayed from the line of march but had not lost his sign:

LET THE HOLY GHOST OUT OF THE CLOSET

51

The Chief was enjoying the ads in *The New Yorker* as his desk clock chimed six. Jeremy came in. "Everyone knows who ought to know," he said. "And everyone knows that if there is a leak, all of them will drown."

"Bring them all in here tomorrow morning, eight sharp. They ought to hear that from me too."

"One thing," Jeremy said. "Randazzo brought it up. Rather agitatedly. Why is Green on the need-to-know list when he's under investigation?"

"Because we need him." Mulvaney opened a leather box and took out a Dunhill cigarette. "Is Green still out there?"

"Yeah. Says he won't leave until you see him."

"You get anything from the note he found on his desk?"

Jeremy shook his head. "The poor bastard is so shook up, he got his own prints all over it."

"This is bad business, Jeremy. Very bad business. Someone pretending to be us. If it caught on, nobody would know whom to be afraid of. Jesus. 'Green, Internal Affairs is on to you.' I want to know who did that. I got to know who did that."

"All right, Jeremy. To start with, how many civilians were up there today before Green showed up? Then there is the possibility that this was a joke by his lamebrained colleagues. If that's what it is, I'll stuff due process up the ass of whoever did it, and I'll break them the minute I find them. God damn it, it's like forging something in the name of the Vatican."

Wilfred Mulvaney felt the red in his face and leaned back a bit in his chair. "I also want to find out what Jeremiah Riordan is doing these days, and with whom."

"You want a tap. A bug?"

"No. Nothing I want to tell a judge. Hell, I don't have anything to tell a judge. I just want a couple of the boys to keep him in view."

Jeremy, moving toward the door, asked, "What are they supposed to be looking for?"

"They are supposed to be keeping him in view. Any other questions?"

"No, sir."

"Okay," Mulvaney got up and shut the window. "Bring in Green. And no calls from anybody. Including the PC."

"And the Mrs."

"If that should come to pass, tell her I'm in with the PC."

Noah Green appeared at the door, his shoulders hunched, his broad face showing hurt, incomprehensions, anger, and fear, all of which he was unsuccessfully trying to mash into a mask of self-assurance. He sat down heavily in a chair across from the Chief's desk.

"I'm on your list, right?" Green was relieved that his voice came out without a crack in it.

Mulvaney coolly contemplated the detective for a few moments before answering. "I would say that you are not far off the mark."

"What? What am I accused of?"

"People are so quick to use that word. I merely want to discuss a few things with you."

"Do I need a lawyer?"

Mulvaney smiled. "I expect you've been asked that by others many, many times. What's your answer?"

Green rubbed his nose. "I tell them, 'I'll give you plenty of warning when and if you need a lawyer. It's to my advantage as well as yours for me to do that.' And then I tell them why."

Mulvaney nodded approvingly. "Shall we proceed?"

Green took out a cigar, looked at Mulvaney, didn't wait for his reaction, and lit it. "It's weird being on the other side of that conversation."

"That's how we grow, Mr. Green, through experience. Well, I'm delighted you came in for a chat. I've heard about you. The painless extractor of confessions. Cuts through all forms of resistance so smoothly that it's only when it's all over they realize the fat lady has just sung."

The Chief carefully removed a manila folder from underneath his desk blotter.

"You taping?" Green asked. "Audio? Video?"

The Chief tapped his forehead. "Just in here. Let us begin. Gudaitis's Bar and Grill on Essex Street, two meetings with Counselor Mendelssohn in the last month that we've seen, and our information is that there have been many such meetings over the years."

"We went to high school together," Green said. "We keep in touch. We meet, we eat, we _shmooze_. I never talk to him about any of his cases, and he never talks to me about them."

"We'll get to that," the Chief said. "During the last meeting, three days ago, at two-twenty in the afternoon, Mendelssohn, while you were in the men's room, put some bills, some currency, in the breast pocket of your jacket. Was that a _shmooze_ or a _shmeer_?"

Green shook his head. "For God's sake, I found him some tapes he wanted for a client. The client is nuts about Kay Kyser, I know all the stores that go way back, and I found him some Kay Kyser."

"Kay Kyser?" Mulvaney looked as if he were about to throw up. "The perversions in this city! Oh, the perversions!"

"I told him I didn't want any money for them. He's a

friend, and besides, if I hadn't been looking for Kay Kyser, I wouldn't have found a Billie Holiday aircheck from Storeyville."

Mulvaney leaned forward. "George Wein's Club in Boston?"

Green nodded.

"Jesus, I heard there were some of those around, but I never saw one."

"I'll make you a dub," Green said.

"Ah, I wish I could say yes but you can understand why I can't. So while you were in the men's room, the counselor disobeyed your wishes and laid some loot on you anyway. How much?"

"Would you believe I didn't know it was there until the cleaner handed it to me yesterday? I never use those pockets. There were five fifty-dollar bills. The tapes cost me about twenty dollars apiece, so that's one hundred dollars. And he had a note on the money saying it was for the baby. Shannon didn't see anything wrong with it, I didn't see anything wrong with it."

"I'm surprised at you," Mulvaney said. "I am really surprised at how somebody as smart as you can come to such a stupid conclusion. I mean smart in self-defense, like we all have to be. Tell me, Detective, you are sitting home watching on television a tape of Mendelssohn depositing this money in the breast pocket of your coat. What the hell does that look like?"

Green sighed. "But it's all explainable."

"Sure. Once that picture is in the mind of John Q. Citizen, you can get God to come down and explain it for all the good it will do you. Never, never do anything you wouldn't want to see, raw, on *60 Minutes*. You get me?"

Green nodded.

Mulvaney looked into the manila folder again. "You remember a case—about four years ago—guy got killed in a fight. Guy's name was Rinaldi. Mike Rinaldi. The accused was—uh—Jack Lundberg. He wound up getting four to eight, manslaughter, though going in, it looked like second-degree murder. You remember that?"

"Yeah, I remember."

"Guy who gets killed is a family man. Guy who kills him is a piece of shit with a record of getting paid for busting heads. So how did it happen? The defense found out something the ADA didn't know. The guy who got killed had been talking of beating the other guy's head in. The defense sprung it—surprise! surprise!—in the middle of the trail, and our side never recovered, even though there was no evidence our guy started what turned out to be his funeral. The question was how come the detective on the case, who knew that information, never told the ADA. And how the defense attorney, who was a close friend of that detective, gets that information? You following me?"

Green nodded.

"Now you might ask, why did the defense attorney, his name was—well, you know his name—why did he give a fuck about this case? He was court-appointed. The punk had no money. None of his sometime employers wanted to be identified with him, so none of them went for a lawyer. So why did Mendelssohn go to the trouble of putting his fine crooked brain to work on this case? Once he got in it, he wanted to win it, of course, by any means necessary. As is his way. But why, Detective, why was he even there?"

"Because the press was watching."

"That's right. A columnist on the *Daily News* had picked it up, decent citizen with a wife and baby at home foully murdered. By a piece of shit. Mendelssohn liked the odds. Nobody thought he could get the guy off. But, if he could get him something so light the whole city would yowl, why, think of the business that would bring."

Mulvaney reached for a Dunhill. "But how the fuck was he going to do it? Well, God is good, God put an old, old friend of his, a detective, on the case, and he went to the detective and asked for help. Nothing serious. Nothing like perjury. Just tell me if you hear something I could use. I'm not saying money was mentioned between those two old friends but what would be wrong if, later on, no matter how the case came out, the counselor gave the detective a couple thou. In case one day he had a baby."

Green flushed. "You want to hear what really happened."

"Well, it says here you filed a report on Mrs. Rinaldi telling you at lunch about her son having had bad thoughts about the piece of shit, only somebody in the DA's office lost the report, you said. Is that what you're going to tell me?"

Green moistened his lips. "I'm sure it also says there, in what you got, that I was drinking then. I was drinking pretty good. I can swear I wrote out a report because the ADA wasn't around that afternoon for me tell him right away. The trial had been recessed because one of the jurors ate some bad shrimp wherever he had lunch and the ADA went off somewhere. Anyway. I wrote it out and I *thought* I'd given it to one of the girls in the office. It's possible that I imagined I did it, and didn't do it. It's possible I was putting them away pretty good at lunch, and I had a pint with me for snacks."

Mulvaney stared at him. "That's not the main question though, Detective. The main question is how Mr. Mendelssohn found out the information to which only you, aside from Rinaldi's parents, were privy."

"He didn't get it from me."

"Oh yes," Mulvaney purred, "that was the year Mendelssohn found Aladdin's lamp. I remember reading about it in *The New York Post*."

"Tell me when you want to listen," Green said.

"I am all ears, Detective."

"Mendelssohn has a secretary. She hates him. That's why he keeps her. It gives him a kick to order someone around who can't stand him."

"Why does she take it?"

"He pays her twice what she could get anywhere else. Anyway, a few weeks after the case was over, I was up there for something, he wasn't around, and she told me that he had two people tail us from day one of the trial. Where we had lunch, they had lunch. And they eavesdropped. If they couldn't get a table next to us, they slipped the waiter enough to make it happen. That's how Mendelssohn found out what he found out."

"That's not in here," Mulvaney pointed to the manila folder. "Whom did you tell that to?"

"No one. I was already enough of a schmuck with that missing report, and I would have been a double schmuck for not having known what was going on at the next table."

"How would you be expected to know?"

"You know the answer to that," Green said. "What I get paid for is being able to smell something funny. Another reason I didn't say anything is he'd know where it came from, and he'd make the secretary suffer. I mean really suffer."

"You're a capital fellow," Mulvaney boomed. "You care about people. The secretary. Yourself. It's only the fucking police force you don't give a shit about. Who knows how many cases that son of a bitch has stolen with his eavesdroppers? Tell me, Detective, was the ADA with you and Rinaldi's parents at any of the lunches?"

"Yeah, one of them."

"In a complaint that will be filed before the bar association, you will testify to that fact, as well as to the presence of eavesdroppers?"

"That woman is still working for him, Chief."

"Are you out of your fucking mind, Green? I thought you came down here because you like wearing that badge."

"Yes, I will do what you want."

"It's what *you* want, Mr. Green. *You* don't want a criminal justice system in which some people have more advantages than others."

Green nodded.

"All right," Mulvaney went on. "Let us assume that you did not sell that information to Mr. Mendelssohn. What were you doing drumming up business for him? Telling Moishe Kagan to hire him. What's the finder's fee these days?"

"I have no apologies for that one," Green said. "The guy was old, the guy was kind of disconnected from what was going on, and all of a sudden he was a murder suspect. He needed a good lawyer."

"That was a very nice fee Mendelssohn was getting from the old man's son. You sure there wasn't something for the baby out of that?"

Green got up. "Listen, if that's the way your mind is going, I'd better get a lawyer myself."

"Sit down, sir, this movie may have a surprise ending."

Green relit his cigar, and sat down.

"Now," Mulvaney looked at him, "you knew of the altercation—the *physical* altercation—between the old man and Blondie. Yet you kept that information from your partner and from you commander. Did you hold it back from Mendelssohn?"

"I never mentioned it to Mendelssohn. I was worried about the old man. If it hit the papers that he and Blondie had had a fight, he could be cleared a million times, but in what was left of his life, he couldn't walk the streets without being pointed at. That's no way to go out. I knew I'd have to tell Dickerson and Randazzo, but I wanted a little time to think about it. Maybe we'd break the case, and the information would be of no use. I dunno, I just felt bad for the old man. And I knew he couldn't have killed that girl. Or any girl. Maybe he could kill a landlord or a boss, but not a couple of whores."

"I forget, where did you do your training in psychiatry? Was it here or abroad?"

"Chief, if I'm worth anything after all these years, I got

to be able to tell who *didn't* do it, even if I don't know who did. However, I was wrong. I should have told about that fight with Blondie right away. Much as I was worried about the old man, I had no business holding out on that stuff."

"When you go home," Mulvaney said, "I want you to go over our entire conversation, except that you will be me. Listen to your answers as if you were me. And then, after you have gone into the toilet, and thrown up in the bowl, go over the conversation again—as me."

Green cleared his throat. "When will I be getting a statement of the charges?"

Mulvaney smiled. "In your dreams, I suppose. Now, I want to talk to you about the case, the bottomless murders."

Green's voice was not entirely under control. "I'm still on it? I'm okay?"

"Barely. This is as far as you go in the department. If the PC wanted, for some reason, to move you up, he could not, not with what I know now. What bothers me most is that you kept your mouth shut in the Rinaldi case about how Mendelssohn got that information. You did not give a shit about what would happen to the secretary. That isn't why you didn't say anything. You didn't want to be humiliated. You didn't want it out that anybody can tune into the big-deal detective while he sits there slurping booze."

Mulvaney stared at Green. "The rest of the stuff is crummy too. Sloppy, self-indulgent, with the department always coming last, or rather, not at all. However, you've not done anything venal, I believe you on that, and I don't want to do without all your experience, including your ability to stroke confessions out of stones. I will consider your role in the complaint to the bar association as partial redemption, minimally partial, for your having messed up the Rinaldi case so good. And I will place a letter in your file, in case I should drop dead. One more thing, Mr. Green. You are drinking beer. Stop it. You hear me?"

Green nodded.

"All right," Mulvaney leaned back and stretched. "I'll get Jeremy in here and we will go over the pitiful amount of material we have on the *Fershtunkiner* cases. Imagine, somebody's got one and a half corpses that belong to us. By the way, you can give me the address of the place where you got that Billie Holiday tape."

52

Although he still walked past it every morning, the stiff-backed black man was surprised to see the newsstand open again a week to the day after it had been closed. The round Jewish man was not there, however. Arranging the papers was a small, dark-skinned woman of about thirty.

"Pardon me," he said, "are you the new owner?"

"Yes," she flashed her teeth at him, "Can I be of any help?"

Mr. Fitzgerald simply picked out his usual papers, paid for them, and went to the phone booth on the corner. Twenty minutes later, sitting in Tompkins Square Park and chuckling in satisfaction at William Safire's column in *The New York Times*, Henry Langston Fitzgerald became aware of a rather large presence in front of him.

"Sit down, Mr. Green," he said.

Noah nodded, took out a cigar, sat, and waited.

"Angel would like to see you," the black man said.

The detective whistled slowly. "That's a relief. I thought he was a goner."

"He's at my place. He has to hide down here because of his mother. There's no one else to look in on her. To get her off the floor, feed her, that sort of thing. No one he trusts. Including me. I offered to. But he says he's got to do it himself. She'd probably bite anybody else. He slips into her place at odd hours. He waits, he looks, he takes chances. I'm surprised they just don't grab her and make him come to them."

Green leaned back on the bench. "She'd make a very unappetizing hostage. And the neighborhood wouldn't like it. Kidnapping a good boy's mother. What does Angel think they think he knows about them?"

"Nothing," Fitzgerald said. "I mean Angel can't figure anything he knows that can do them any harm. He knows what people on the street know, that's about it. But they're not sure that's all he knows and he figures that if they ever get him, that's going to make them very angry, that they've wasted all this time on him."

"Smoke," Green muttered. "Everybody's walking in smoke."

A schnauzer advanced on Green and barked at him with passionate distaste.

"Fucking anti-Semite," the detective said. "You notice," he turned to Fitzgerald, "whom he came up to. Where do I see Angel?"

"Would you like to come by this afternoon? About four? The Bowery. Three-forty. Top floor. What kind of jam do you like?"

"I'm not particular," Green said.

"The man who used to own the newsstand," the black man said, "is he all right?"

"Not exactly. He doesn't go out of the house. He doesn't talk on the phone. He sits."

"They've tried medication?"

"He won't take it," the detective said. "He says there's nothing to get better for."

The black man rubbed his chin. "Do you think I might visit him?"

"He won't see anybody. I went out there and sat with his wife for a while, but he wouldn't come out of his room."

"Well," Fitzgerald got on his feet, "if you'd be good

enough to give me the address anyway. I have plenty of time, and I have something he needs."

"What's that?"

"Jesus Christ."

"Oh boy," Green kept a straight face. "That's just the ticket. That's just the medicine he needs." Green wrote out the address. "If he won't come out, yell in what you have for him. Then he'll come out. Oh yes."

53

He was breathing too hard, so he stopped on the third floor. *Suppose I was chasing somebody up these fucking stairs. Hell of a thing. New baby, and his old man dies of a heart attack. I had no business being a father at such an age in the first place. But then, to keep on being a fucking fat slob with the pastrami sandwiches and the onion rings. No more. No more. No more delicatessen. No more ice cream. Carrots, raw carrots all day long. Kid, I'll be at your graduation. From elementary school anyway.*

Cheered up, Green, still breathing heavily, made it up to the sixth floor, stopped at the black door, read the scripture, and knocked.

Angel opened the door, his eyes full of fear. "Jesus, man, you want a doctor? Or an ambulance? Sit down, Noah."

Embarrassed, Green sat down and took a glass of water from the stiff-backed black man, who then set alongside him a tray with scones, raspberry jam, and a pot of tea on it. "Just a little indigestion," the detective finally said as the black man left the room.

"The guy they sent after me," Angel was pacing, "may be the guy you want. The carver. I don't have anything hard but he once told me he works for them, kind of a trouble-shooter, and he's got ice in his eyes. If anybody could have cut them in two like that without being crazy, he's the guy."

"What makes you think whoever did it isn't crazy?" Green burped and felt a lot better.

"I figured it out, I think," Angel stopped and turned toward the detective. "It was neat the way they made it look, but when you really look at it, the pieces don't fit. Okay, two whores, but why was Sol's kid the third one? The murderer's an AC-DC nut? Maybe, but there was a better explanation. I knew about the busts of their people and that a lot of merchandise got taken because somebody—you or the feds—had gotten on the inside. So they had to send out the word about what happens to snitches.

"But," Angel sat down opposite Green, "but the message was just for snitches. They'd know. A snitch can smell another snitch dead or alive. But to the outside, to the straights, to the press, they didn't want to look like Al Capone. They didn't want any attention coming to them for what happened to the three snitches. It's bad for business, and God forbid, they might get their own pictures in the papers. So they make it look, to the outside, like a nut took care of those three, like it had nothing to do with anything else. Just a nut who can't stand it that Thanksgiving comes just once a year.

"They figured," Angel watched Green who remained impassive, "you guys and the feds might stumble on to what happened sooner or later. But by then, the press would be on to new blood, and this would be played like just another rubout. A one-day story. No pictures. And they also figured that if you figured out it was a contract, you'd figure the pro came in from out of town, and cut out again as soon as he'd checked off the last one on his list. So where to look for him? Could be anywhere? Colombia? Bolivia? Could be an Israeli. They're the toughest dudes there ever was, from what I hear. And even if you found the guy, they figured he wouldn't talk. The kind of pro they'd get would never talk. Not fear, man. Pride.

"So whichever way it goes, they got the messages out to the snitches, and nobody knows who the fuck *they* are. The ones who got no names, no offices, no reflections in the mirror, you know. Maybe they never even *been* here themselves, you ever figure that? Maybe right now they're sitting in Macao, looking forward to the end of the business day so they can go home and be with their wives and kids. Maybe everything they make happen over here is just something on a computer printout to them. You know what I'm talking about? None of it's real to them. The two whores. Sol's kid. You. Me."

"One step at a time," Green said. "They guy who went after you. Tell me about him."

"I don't know if he was supposed to just bring me in," Angel said, "or bring me down. He had this big fucker of a knife, but maybe that was just to scare me into going with him."

"His name? Do you know his name?"

"Arthur. Tall, skinny, almost white. He's a runner, a jogger."

"That Arthur?" Green smiled with anticipation.

"Yeah, he says you busted him once, but you screwed it up."

"My people have a saying, Angel. 'Never again.' So you think he might be the carver."

"I'm trying to think the way they think," Angel was pacing again. "There's an obvious advantage in importing someone. He's in and out so fast none of you guys have any idea what he looks like. But in a situation like this, when they're not sure how many snitches screwed them, the killings will take time, so you might as well use someone you can get hold of right away whenever you need him. Someone you know is dependable, someone with ice in his eyes."

Green nodded.

"And," Angel went on, "Arthur's got a cute cover. He runs every day, no matter what. Everybody sees him running. Would somebody like that carve people up and put their heads in a garbage can? He's so clean he could be in a TV ad, him in his white shorts and dignified sneakers."

Green took out a small black notebook. "Angel, the knife. How long was that knife, the one Arthur had when he was coming after you?"

"Got to have been a six-to eight-inch blade. One of them gravity knives, you know."

Green got up. "Where would I go looking for Arthur?"

"In about an hour, he'll be jogging past Tompkins Square Park."

"What about after?"

"He usually eats in Café Loup, East Thirteenth, near Fifth. Around eight. None of the restaurants in this neighborhood are good enough for Arthur."

"Angel," Green put a hand on the youngster's shoulder, "these chances you're taking seeing your mother. That's not smart. I can get her into a hospital."

"NO, MAN!" Angel shouted. "People like my mother go into a hospital, they die there. No, you leave her to me."

The straight-backed black man reappeared and showed Green to the door, asking, "Are you going to arrest that Arthur?"

"Just for openers," the detective said.

54

At quarter to eight that evening, Angel and Green were in a car at Fourteenth Street and Broadway. "You wait until he leaves, right?" Green said. "You're on the other side of the street. If he doesn't see you, give him a whistle. Then you run, hollering, toward University Place. You can out-sprint him, and this ain't going to be no marathon. If he doesn't take his knife out, ask him where the hell it is, did somebody take it away from him. You know how to do it. Ask him if he's afraid he'll cut himself."

"What if he's not carrying the knife?" Angel was trying to keep his hands still.

"I'll get him anyway. I see what you're thinking. I'll get him before he bangs you. But we've lost him if the motherfucker doesn't have the knife. At least we've lost him this time."

They left the car, walked up Fourteenth Street to University Place where Angel went the rest of the way alone to Café Loup and went inside. Green waited in a doorway across the street. The store was dark. Green settled himself on the ground, put a paper bag with a half-empty bottle of rum in it next to him, and then placed his hat over his face.

A few minutes later, a miniature schnauzer, with the nastily clacking bark common to all members of that breed, started to sniff the supine detective.

"Get away from there!" a woman snapped. "God knows

what kind of diseases you'll pick up from that filthy bum. They ought to throw him in the garbage can where he belongs."

"HE'S GONNA KILL ME! HE'S GONNA KILL ME! HELP!" Angel's voice, its fear not in the least simulated, pierced the soft evening air.

Green, on his feet, kicking the dog away, saw Angel screaming down Thirteenth Street with Arthur close behind. There was nothing in Arthur's hands.

Green ran toward them, drew his gun, shouted, "FREEZE, ARTHUR!" He pushed Arthur against a store window, yanked his arms behind him, handcuffed him, and patted him down.

"Inside the shirt," Angel said.

Green was afraid there'd be nothing there but underwear. He broke into a big smile when he saw the knife, which he carefully removed, blade first, from its thin cloth sheath that had been attached to a strap around Arthur's chest. Green took a paper bag from his pocket, removed a smaller paper bag from inside, and put the knife, holding it blade first, into the larger bag.

"A man can carry a knife," Arthur said smoothly. "I wasn't even holding it. I was just chasing a kid who called me a faggot as I'm leaving a restaurant. That's a fighting word, Jew. Look it up in the law books. You're going to be the schmuck of the week if you bring me in just for chasing a kid."

Green stood in front of Arthur and, with a flourish, took a laminated card from his shirt pocket. "Sir, listen good, I am about to read you your rights. If there is anything you do not understand, I shall be pleased to repeat them."

The detective cleared his throat.

"You have the right to remain silent.

"Anything you say can be used against you in a court of law.

"You have the right to the presence of an attorney to assist you prior to questioning and to be with you during questioning if, sir, you so desire."

Green took on a compassionate drone. "If you cannot afford an attorney, you have the right to have an attorney appointed for you prior to questioning. Do you understand these rights?"

Arthur smiled, and said nothing.

"Would you like to hear them in Yiddish?" Green asked.

"I already have," Arthur said.

"Will you voluntarily answer my questions?"

"I liked the third item on the menu," Arthur looked at Green. "The one about the lawyer prior to questioning. When I make that call, what shall I tell my lawyer the charge is?"

Green took a sheet of notepaper from his pants pocket, and read:

"Local Law No. 64 (of 1983), Section b.—"It shall be unlawful for any person to carry on his or her person or have in his or her possession, in any public place, street or park any knife which has a blade length of four inches or more."

"What do you get for that?" Arthur asked. "A letter to your mama?"

"Fifteen days," the detective said.

Arthur delicately snorted. "What do you think you can do with me in fifteen days?"

Green pushed Arthur in the direction of the car.

A couple of hours later, as Angel was leaving the precinct house, he said to Green, "How are you going to get anywhere if his lawyer's always going to be around?"

"Even lawyers got to sleep. I can't question Arthur without the lawyer there, but if Arthur wants to just talk to me, about any old thing but the murders, I'm not going to refuse to be neighborly. I know what it is to be lonely and need somebody to talk to. And you, kid, you're not out of the woods yet."

"Huh?"

"They hire Arthur, they can hire somebody else. You get the picture? Watch yourself at all times."

55

"**H**ow did you know about her?" Randall Dickerson asked as he looked out in the darkness, at the trees in front of the precinct house.

"I found her when I pulled in Arthur before. She didn't want anything to do with him. Wouldn't talk to me, wouldn't see him. It was like a very late abortion."

"So what do you figure is different now?"

"I got a hunch. Arthur may have gone too far for her to keep pretending he died."

"You going to call?"

Green shook his head. "No. If I'm at her door, she can't hang up on me. I got to do this fast, in a slow way. We only have fifteen days, and if she won't help, I'll have to find another way. If we have to let him go, we'll never see him again."

"Arthur's not that inconspicuous," Dickerson was still watching the kids outside.

"He will be—where they put him."

"He must know that'll happen to him if he gets out."

Green stretched. "Arthur is convinced he's smarter than everybody. He figures he'll be able to stay alive by disappearing. For good. He also feels hurt, if that's possible, that they don't realize he would never tell us who hired him to do the carving. He could put him on the rack and he wouldn't say a fucking word."

"How come you're so sure of what goes on in Arthur's head?" Dickerson asked.

"I think about Arthur a lot," Green said, buttoning his shirt collar and pulling up his tie. "Okay, time to see his mama."

Green drove down to Rivington Street and parked in front of a tenement. He walked up to the third floor, and just as he was going to knock, Green heard a strong, deep voice singing. The sound was penetrating, but not loud.

> *"Softly and tenderly*
> *Jesus is calling.*
> *Calling for you and for me.*
> *Calling, 'Oh, sinner, come home.'"*

Green had to beat down an urge to go back downstairs. Not because of the music. His hand had touched a dark crucifix on the door.

The detective knocked gently. He heard her moving toward the door.

"Yes," the deep voice said.

"Mrs. Heath," Green said, "I'm Detective Green, New York City Police Department. I'd very much appreciate your help, if I could come in for a moment."

One bolt was drawn, and in a crack in the door appeared a face made of mahogany. Her hair, straight and thin, was white, and her eyes were a deep, shining brown.

"Identification," she said.

Green put his badge up to the crack.

"What precinct?"

"Ninth."

"What street is it on?"

"East Fifth."

"Put your eyes right up to where I can see them."

Green, remembering a colleague who had stopped being

able to read after having had lye thrown at him in a similar situation, hesitated. And then did what he had been told.

"All right," she said. Two more bolts were drawn and the door was opened. In the center of the room was a square table, with four chairs. There was no other furniture. The room opened into a bedroom where all Green could see was a cot and a blanket. He wondered where the pillows were, but then decided there weren't any.

On the table was a Bible bound in what, to the horrified detective, looked like human skin.

Mrs. Heath, tall, angular, with high cheekbones and a wisp of hair coming down from her chin, picked up the Bible and handed it to Green.

"It's not what you think," she said with a chill smile. "That is pigskin. It wears very well. Certainly a police detective knows the difference between human skin and pigskin. I assume you want to talk to me about Arthur. Yes, I remember you. Not the name. I did not remember the name. But I remember your eyes. Anyway, I thought I had made myself quite clear last time. Whatever maternal feelings I might have had for that person disappeared a long, long time ago. And I do not practice sentimentality. Nor do I practice fantasy. Whatever is wrong with Arthur cannot be fixed."

Mrs. Heath went into the bedroom and returned with a round, red, tin container. Inside was an assortment of cookies. She handed the tin to Green who cautiously chose one and kept it in his hand.

She looked at his hand.

"I'll keep it for later," Green said, "after I eat."

"Do you have any children?" Mrs. Heath asked.

"One. Though," he dutifully added, "I also have a stepson, my wife's."

"Whose else?" Mrs. Heath said. "Having one that's really your own, you probably won't understand this, but I would be so happy, so very happy, if you came tonight to tell me that Arthur is dead. Did you?"

"No," Green took out a cigar, but didn't light it.

"No," she said. "This is my home, and the stench would last for a week."

"No, Arthur isn't dead. I came because we have reason to believe Arthur may be involved in a series of murders. Not drugs or prostitution like last time, but murder. So far, two young women and a young man have been killed. In each case, the corpses—I'm sorry to have to tell you this—"

"Perfectly all right," Mrs. Heath took a cookie from the red tin container, "I am not a delicate person."

"The corpses were cut in two. The heads and the upper part of the bodies were left in garbage cans. So far, we have not been able to recover the—"

"Lower regions," Mrs. Heath put the cookie in her mouth. "And you think," she stared at Green, "that I can persuade Arthur to confess."

"That is my hope. So long as Arthur is out there, there's no one he's not capable of murdering, one way or another."

"Including his mother," Mrs. Heath said dryly.

"Except his mother."

"What makes you so sure?" Mrs. Heath seemed about to smile.

"The last time," Green said, "the few people I was able to find who knew Arthur before he left home, all of them said he was afraid of you. No, the word was 'terrified.'"

Mrs. Heath got up from the table, went into her bedroom, and from there into another room. Following her, Green saw an ancient black stove, a tin kettle, a cupboard, a small round table, and a single chair. There was a Bible on the table.

"Tea or coffee?" she asked.

"Coffee. Black."

"I knew you'd be trouble when I looked into your eyes out there. Soft. They look soft. But way down, there's a coldness. Nothing stops you. All to the good so far as that Arthur is concerning." She set a cup in front of Green. There were letters on it. BROOKLYN DODGERS.

"Yes, he was afraid of me," she said, watching the kettle. "And if he was terrified as well, it was of the void. The emptiness, where I was supposed to be. Arthur wanted me to be to him what other mothers were to their children. And I was at first. Oh yes. I took him everywhere with me, everywhere. I can still see how intently he would watch in church. I didn't know who was looking out of those eyes. But when he started going to school, I knew, all too soon, that he was Satan's child. From then on, I had all I could do to put food in front of him."

"By Satan's child, you mean—"

"Oh for goodness sake," Mrs. Heath poured the coffee into the cup in front of Green, "I don't mean Satan impregnated me. I mean the boy was wicked. Surely, you, a policeman, understand what I mean. I took him to preachers and social workers and even to psychiatrists, and most of them said the same thing. The honest ones. They said, 'Mrs. Heath, there are some people who are beyond our help. They are just plain wicked. Not just bad. Wicked. Therapy will not do them any good. Medication will not do them any good.' It is foolish to use such terms as neurosis or psychosis or chemical imbalance when you're confronted by such people. They are Satan's children. They are wicked."

Green looked into his cup. "Having come to that conclusion, you—"

"I gave him food and clothes and a place to sleep. Period. And he, he, as he got older, started jawing about 'love.' Why, that boy didn't know any more about love than an alligator. He had heard the word, and then he'd read about the word, and he decided he was entitled to whatever it was because he was a child. But there is no way to love the truly wicked. Sinners, yes. You can condemn the sin, but not the sinner. But a sinner knows he has sinned. The truly wicked do not know they have sinned."

She was standing next to the stove, no longer looking at Green. She was in another time. "Nobody would come home with him to play, because they heard what happened to those who did." She shivered. "And I, because he was so quiet, didn't know what was going on. Until their mothers complained. Oh, how they complained. The boys had been afraid to do or say anything because he told them what else he would do to them if they said anything. But finally, they told their mothers. Not their fathers."

"When did this start?" Green asked.

"The buggering? What does it matter? You don't understand. The wicked *are* wicked. There's nothing chronological about it. They don't *become* wicked. Some children bite in kindergarten. So did Arthur. But Arthur was biting children in the fourth grade. He would have buggered them in kindergarten too if he could have, if he'd had the equipment. Maybe he did. Well, I've told you just a small part of my life with Arthur. Buggering was only one of his vocations. But that's enough for now."

Green drank some coffee. "Mrs. Heath, you could be a great deal of help to us if you were to come visit Arthur. Right now, if that's at all possible."

"What will happen to Arthur if he confesses?" Mrs. Heath's deep voice grew deeper.

"He'll be in for life. I mean a real life sentence. Many more years than he can possibly live."

"I wouldn't be too sure of that," she said. "Very well. I am prepared to see my son."

56

His eyes closed, he was running in place, a very long run this evening, all the way west to Washington Square Park and now, he figured, it was such a balmy night, he might as well keep on until he came to the river. But that was not to be.

He opened his eyes.

"I used to feel your presence quite a distance away," Arthur said to the tall, angular woman with white hair. "But not until this moment did I know you were here."

"I must be losing my powers," she said, standing in front of the cell, beyond hand's reach.

"They didn't bring you a chair. They must know you never tire."

She smiled.

"It won't work," Arthur said, smiling in turn.

"You can always tell me to go," Mrs. Heath folded her arms across her chest.

"No, I won't do that."

"You did it once before, Arthur."

"That's why I shall never do it again."

Neither spoke for several minutes. Arthur began to run again. "Are you wired, Mother?" he asked.

"You know me, son. Nothing is hidden. Ever."

"Oh, I wouldn't say that," Arthur said, running faster.

She watched him run. She watched for a long time.

"Do you believe what they told you about me, Mother?" Arthur said, slackening his pace.

"I want to know whether *you* believe it, Arthur."

He laughed. "Answer my question first."

Her hands still folded, she said, "I have known for a long time that there is nothing of which you are not capable. So there is nothing they could say that would be difficult for me to believe."

"Why do you want to do their work for them, Mother? But then you never acted much like a mother. Except for that time."

She leaned against the wall. "You were twenty-four years old, and I bathed you. Or started to."

Arthur shook his head. "I never did know who told you I had that fever and all, but I woke up, and—"

"And told me to get the fuck out."

"I was delirious, that's all. You should have known that. I didn't know it was you. I didn't know who it was. It could have been one of the whores. That's who I thought it was."

"Actually, I was the one who was delirious. One of your playmates told me you were dying, and I quite forgot who you were. All I had in my head was that my son was dying."

"If you had had that in your head, the son part, a long time before—" Arthur stopped.

His mother smiled without mirth. "Finish it. You would have been such a different person. Bullshit. You are the only person I've ever known without a soul. It was just left out when you were made."

"You were there, Mother. Who else was?"

Her smile grew wider. "I wish I knew, Arthur. I wasn't there at all."

Arthur grabbed the bars. "What the hell are you saying?"

"I made a promise when I took you. I made a promise to Him that you would never know that you were not mine. I kept that promise, no matter what you did. The stealing, the lying, the violence, the viciousness, the way you put your penis into anything it could fit into, and things it couldn't, the buying and selling of women and men and boys and drugs and God knows what. Well, He knows everything you have done, although I've been spared some of it. Still, I never said, to you or anyone else, that you were not mine. But I have talked with Him, and He says it is not right any longer for you to believe you are mine. You must know the truth about yourself."

Sitting on a chair, Arthur stared at her.

"She was a whore," Mrs. Heath moved closer to the bars. "She thought a good deal of herself though, and she carried herself that way. She was light. Light enough to pass if the sun wasn't too strong. She liked doing tricks, she said, because you never knew who was coming. When she found out you were coming, she was going to have you killed, but I said to her, 'Have the baby, and I'll take care of it.' I was so proud of myself. I had saved a baby from being murdered. God help me."

"What was her name?"

"Flossie."

"Sounds like a dog. What happened to her?"

"Gone. She just went. Somewhere. I never heard from her again. Nobody else I knew did either."

"You don't know if she's dead or alive?"

"No."

Arthur got up and went to the bars. "And my father?"

"She never knew who he was. She never knew which one he was. The streets are full of people who could have been your father."

"You told me he was a teacher, a math teacher, who was going to marry you but he died just before I was born."

"Well, if I told you one lie, I could tell you two, and I did."

Arthur turned his back on her.

"I cannot believe it," she said softly, "he thinks he can cry."

"Good-bye, *Mother,*" Arthur said to the wall.

She looked at him sitting straight. She lifted her chin and walked away. In the squadroom, she refused a chair, and told Green what had happened.

Green looked at her, and said, "You *are* his natural mother?"

"Of course," Mrs. Heath said.

57

An hour later, Green, reading the comic strips in the *Daily News* and smoking a cigar, walked past Arthur's cell.

The prisoner was standing next to, but not touching, the bars. He was humming softly. Some kind of hymn, Green thought.

"In case you were wondering," Green said, "we didn't think you'd be safe at Riker's. Word's out you're in, somebody may get nervous. So we'll look after you here."

"Tell me something I don't know."

Green moved on to "Gasoline Alley."

"Jew," Arthur said, "what's around the corner?"

"A cop."

"That's all?"

"That's all. Want me to send him away?"

"How do I know he's away?"

"You can look."

"Just you and me," Arthur said.

"That's right."

"Do it."

Green walked around the corner where a uniformed officer at a desk was reading the personals in *The Village Voice*.

"You never know what you'll catch from that sort of stuff," Green said, "I wouldn't even touch the paper. The prisoner maybe wants to talk, but private. Give me the keys, and get yourself some coffee."

The cop nodded, gave Green the keys, and left. Green picked up the phone on the desk, spoke briefly, and hung up.

The cop came back. "Sure you don't want me to stick around?"

"No thanks," Green said, "I just got me some backup."

Green came back to the cell and unlocked it. Arthur walked out, stopped in front of Green, walked past him, looked around the corner, and came back.

"I just want to talk some," Arthur said. "No lawyer. Just you and me. You shook me up, bringing her in, just like you wanted to."

"You could say in court I made you talk, and they could throw out everything you're about to tell me. They could throw it out anyway because I know you've got a lawyer, and he's not here. A judge could say that no matter what you want, you shouldn't be talking without your lawyer being here. Who the hell knows anymore what a judge could say? I'm trying to figure out what's in your finely tuned mind, Arthur."

"You're worrying about nothing. I'm crazy."

"That's a much harder defense to make these days, Arthur."

"You want to know what happened to the other halves of those bodies?" Arthur grinned.

Green remained silent.

"I ate them."

"Just what I thought," Green said.

"You want to know who gave me the contract?"

Green waited.

"Jesus," Arthur said.

"I didn't know he was living in Macao these days."

Arthur laughed. "You had better be funning, Jew. Hey," Arthur's eyes left Green's and went past him. "You said we'd be all alone!"

Green turned, Arthur leapt on him and pressed a short, sharp knife against his windpipe.

Through the fear and pain, Green was thinking, *The oldest fucking trick in the book, and I fell for it. Oy, a Yiddishe kopf!*

"Listen very carefully," Arthur crooned into his ear. "If I slit your windpipe, you will bleed to death before you know it, let alone before anyone else knows it."

"Where'd you have it?" Green choked out the words.

"Trade secret."

"Up your ass."

"Which one?" Arthur pressed the blade in harder. "You made her tell that lie to break me," he said. "It is a lie, right?"

"I don't know what you're talking about." Green began to gag as Arthur jammed the handle of the knife against his windpipe.

"You made her say I'm not her son," Arthur said. "You made her say I'm a whore's son."

Choking, Green was just barely able to say, "I don't know what the fuck you're talking about."

"Drop it," Randall Dickerson said, "or it's good-bye Arthur."

"That's what I'm saying, nigger," Arthur yelled. There was a beat of silence, and Green saw a bullet smash into the hand holding the knife. Green heard two other shots, saw blood spurt onto his shirt and pants, and heard, as if from a great distance, Arthur's disappearing voice, "It is not true. It is not true. Oh, Jesus is calling for you and me, Oh yes, Oh yes-s-s—"

Shaking his head, Green started to rise, fell on Arthur's chest, shivered, rose again, and held himself against the wall. He wanted to throw up, but held it.

Randall looked down at Arthur. "Now that's good shooting. You see what happened? When he said, 'That's what I'm saying, nigger,' he waited to see how I'd take that. Not only the nigger part, but did I dig what he was saying. Good-bye, Arthur, good-bye, Noah. That gave me just enough time. I got the hand with the knife so he couldn't take you to Jesus with him, and then I got the whole motherfucker."

Green put his hand on Dickerson's shoulder.

"You said it," Dickerson put his hand on Green's. "No more need be said."

"Ain't no words," Green said. "But anything you ever need."

"I'll think of something."

"Very nice," Captain Fortunato Randazzo had been standing in the corridor and now moved to where he could get an unimpeded view of the corpse. "Very nice. Now we're back where we started from. No confession. So we'll never know for sure he did all that carving. And if he did, who paid him."

Randazzo looked at Dickerson and snapped, "You couldn't shoot to disable?"

"You mean hit him in the kneecap?" Dickerson said, "while he finished the job on Noah?"

Randazzo grunted. "There are ways, God damn it. The feds are going to love this. We had the key and we broke it." Randazzo sighed.

"One thing," he turned to Green. "Let me see if I can get this through the olive oil in my brain. You took away his mama to break him, right? *Then* what was going to happen?"

"I figured," Green said, "he might fall apart and talk his head off because nothing would mean anything to him anymore. Or he might get so fucking angry that he'd take it out on me because I got his mama into the act. No way he was going to hurt his mama, so it would have to be me. Once he lost control that way, I'd have him. He'd have to let something out."

"You know something," Randazzo said, "scumbag of the

world that he was, that was a terrible thing to do, bringing his mama into this, the way you did it. Unless it worked, which it didn't."

Green struggled to keep his voice even. "It could have worked. And for all they know out there, it did work."

Randazzo sighed again. "We're still back where we started from. Goddamn Arthur fucked us good the last time he could."

58

At noon, two days later, in Randazzo's office, Green, Dickerson, and the captain were looking anywhere but at each other.

"Well," Green said, "at least the press isn't asking any questions. Prisoner grabs a detective to deal his way out and he gets shot. One-day story, one-subject story."

Randazzo grunted. "They haven't made any connection, but they're still asking about those bodies without bottoms. So's the PC. I told the PC we think we had the guy, hell, we know we had the guy, all right, we almost know, and you know what he told me?"

No one volunteered.

"He told me everything I've done on this case I should put into a folder and stick in where the sun don't shine. I thought he was a cultivated man, that asshole."

The phone rang. Randazzo listened, hung up, and said, "Mrs. Heath. She's got something for us. Where the hell's my tape recorder? Oh yeah. I got a feeling we're about to start looking good in our usual way—by holding out our hands."

The tall, composed woman came into the office and nodded at Green who introduced her to the captain and Dickerson. She took a small package out of her pocketbook, unwrapped it, held up a cassette, and gave it to Randazzo who also reached for the wrapping, and then popped the cassette into the tape recorder on the desk.

"It came in the mail this morning," Mrs. Heath said, her deep voice as smooth as glass. "There was a note with it." She took a piece of paper out of her large black handbag, and gave it to Randazzo. "He says—he said—that he left instructions to have this sent to me in the event of his untimely death. He dates the note and the tape. He made it two weeks ago." She sat back, folded her hands, and looked at Randazzo.

"Before this and before the time you came to see him here," Randazzo asked, "when was the last time you heard from him?"

"I get a card every Mother's Day and on my birthday. Also on his birthday," Mrs. Heath pursed her lips.

"That's it?" Randazzo said.

"That's it, ever since he left home. Let's see, he's thirty-one, so that means sixteen years of these syrupy cards. Actually, he didn't leave home. I told him, after he had buggered a child, a retarded child, Gold help us, I told him that if he ever stepped in that door again, I would split open his head with a meat cleaver. He knew I meant it."

Randazzo rubbed his nose, pulled his ear, and said, "You never sent him for help?"

"Oh please. God knows how many psychiatrists wrote papers about Arthur on my money. Well, I thought you might want to hear the tape."

Randazzo nodded, and started the machine.

"Mother," the voice was light and musical, with a slight lilt, "I am now dead, or you would not be hearing this. I am delighted to have pleased you at last. But I could not leave without a last attempt at explaining myself. You never had the patience to listen, to really listen, before. You will listen now because no one can resist paying attention to a voice from the grave."

All the listeners were impassive, except for Captain Randazzo who, with a grin, lunged for the apothecary jar and removed a clump of sourballs.

"My first memory," the voice went on, "is of being in a carriage. You were not there. A boy looked into the carriage, poked me hard in the eye, poked me hard in the nose, and then grabbed my penis hard. When you came back, I tried to tell you what had happened. You laughed."

"Nonsense," Mrs. Heath snapped.

"In school, at first, I was the beanbag. I was sat on, thrown across the room, even peed on. Then one day, this beanbag suddenly grew claws and choked a boy into a state of terror. I had never known a feeling like that. It was delicious. It was delicious all over. There is no other pleasure like it. I have felt it many, many times since, and it is always like the first time.

"I shall spare you what you know, and what you do not know, of the rest of my life, except for certain events of recent weeks. I am sure you have heard of the three corpses found in garbage cans. Or rather the halves of three corpses. In a sense, Mother, they were presents from me to you. I sent those filthy souls to your God before they could defile this world any more. Two whores and a Jewish fag. Have I not left the world at least that much better off? Consider the foul diseases I have saved untold numbers from. God, when He cared for this world, would smite whole cities of the wicked. My powers are limited, but I have made a contribution.

"In honesty, Mother, and I have always been honest with you, my work as God's helper had another purpose, and another kind of reward. Those three were informers, and as a highly skilled craftsman in these matters, I was engaged for a handsome fee to make sure they would sing no more. I tell you, Mother, with each of them, it was like being back in kindergarten, the first time I knew I had claws.

"Now, I know you will be listening to this, if not for the first time, in the company of members of the police department. You have always done your duty. Tell them to put away their pencils for this tape is ending and will not include any information whatever about my employer in my final labor of everlasting love. My refusal to be a snitch—a term of the trade, Mother—is both a matter of principle and more pleasurably, a pardonable act of terminal self-indulgence. I mean the delightful adieu of denying the police department what it most wants—a golden key to the entire operation. So fuck you, gentlemen, especially the Jew, Green.

"And Mother, good-bye. I have been more wicked, much more wicked, than you can possibly imagine, and it's all because of you, Mother. It's all because of you. Sweet dreams, Mother. Jesus is calling. Calling for you and for me. Calling, 'Oh, sinner come home.' Jesus wants a blow job, Mother. I can hardly wait."

The voice was gone. Mrs. Heath's arms were folded.

"That is your son's voice?" Randazzo looked at her.

"Yes," she said.

"You will sign a statement to that effect?"

"Yes. Do you have any further need of me after I sign the statement?"

"Not at the moment," Randazzo said. "Thank you so much for bringing in the tape, and for everything you've done."

"He's right," Mrs. Heath said to no one in particular. "I can't begin to imagine how wicked he was. If I'd only known, I'd have killed him before he came into the world. God would have forgiven me."

"Tell me," Randazzo asked, "what about the burial?"

"Burn him," Mrs. Heath said, "and flush him down the toilet. Keep flushing until you are sure that every bit of him is gone."

59

"They checked me out," the stiff-backed black man was saying at a back table of a Chinese restaurant in Queens. "They need another messenger. They checked where I used to work, and what I've been doing since. That didn't take long. And they said if I ever opened a package, they would open me. And they said if I ever disappeared with a package, they would make sure it would be for good."

Green, playing with a cigar, looked at the spry old man. "They speak the truth."

"I like being useful," Henry Langston Fitzgerald said. "That's why I am a Christian. I had been thinking of getting married again because I was not using all my time to its best advantage, but this is work that truly has to be done and I could not subject a new bride to this much worry."

Green poured tea for the two of them. "You're a hell of a guy. Well, be very careful, and then be more careful. I'll let you know the next place we'll meet. It'll never be the same place. If you have to call, use this number," Green gave him a sheet of notepaper. "Ask for Minister Granger or Minister McEnvoy. Doesn't matter, so long as you say, 'Minister.' Tell him you want to check an interpretation of scripture, and give him a couple of lines. We'll get in touch with you right away. Okay?"

Fitzgerald nodded. "What if there's an emergency?"

"I was coming to that. Ask for Minister whoever and say it's about a christening. Give the address of the parents, which is where you are at that moment. Another thing. Keep a record of where you go for them, the names of the companies or the people that get the packages, anything else you think useful, and mail that record—do not keep a copy—to this name and address."

Green pushed another sheet of notepaper across the table. On it was written: Ben Greenbaum, c/o Jews Who Have Found Jesus, 118 Myrtle Street, New York, NY 10011.

"Have they really?" Fitzgerald leaned forward.

"Not these," Green said. "It's just a safe address. It's a real office though, with literature and all that stuff in case anybody comes in off the street."

"What happens then?"

"Our guys give them a spiel and hand out the pamphlets. It's a free country."

Green speared the last fried dumpling. "If they ever ask you to mail anything, memorize what you can of the envelope. And again, you are a hell of a guy. We appreciate it."

"I'll tell you the main reason I'm doing this," Fitzgerald said. "It was a terrible thing that happened to Sol. More terrible than what happened to his son, because Sol is still living. All those years, I never said much to Sol, but he was part of my life. He was always there. You get old, you appreciate people who are always there, who know you, even if the only thing they know is what papers you take. I never heard him say anything mean to anybody or about anybody. So, it won't help Sol a lot, but maybe it'll help him a little if we get these people."

Green got up. "Stay here awhile. And stay well."

60

Angel, bopping down Avenue C on a bright Sunday morning, had just about decided on going to law school after he finished at City College. And then politics. And then the bench, a seat on the Second Circuit, and then, at fifty-two or fifty-four, the Supreme Court. The first Puerto Rican on the high court. He grinned. *You know what will really shake them up? I'm going to take the oath bilingual.*

"Holy Jesus!" Barely visible under a not quite closed garbage can was an ear, a most unpleasant ear, even if it weren't in a garbage can.

"Not again!" Angel whispered as he took a piece of newspaper from the gutter and used it to lift the lid. On top, cushioned on a mound of peppers and beans, was the head of a pig.

Angel almost leaned over and kissed the pig's head, put back the cover, and whistling, went on his way.

61

Wilfred Mulvaney was deeply engrossed in deciding what to have for lunch. Having hit upon a chef's salad with Irish bread and a Heineken's, he was feeling nicely virtuous as Jeremy knocked. "Captain Riordan," Jeremy said.

"Send him in." Mulvaney sat up straight at his desk.

Riordan, his white hair long in the back, came in and put out his hand. Mulvaney ignored the hand, and also kept the old cop standing.

"You filed a false report with Internal Affairs," Mulvaney said brusquely. "And you didn't have the balls to put your name on it."

Riordan put his fingers together. "I don't know what you mean."

"Knock it off, Jeremiah. You were trying to get Green any way you could, and it was all smoke. IAD isn't for vendettas, and it's not for anti-Semites."

"It was all in good faith," Riordan said loudly. "Everything I gave you was true. I didn't put my name on it so you'd really look at it, God damn it!"

"Everything can be true and at the same time be so incomplete that it's a lie. You didn't give one fuck for the department. You wanted to get the Jew. You wanted him so bad you had your lady friend lie to a detective so she could get a chance to slip your lousy note on Green's desk."

"You got it wrong," Riordan's face was now quite red. I don't know what you're talking about."

Mulvaney stared at him. "You stupid Mick. Her prints are on it. The old bag's a bunco artist. She didn't tell you, Jeremiah? Once we got the mug shot, one of our boys made her. At Rafferty's. With you."

"The woman you are defaming is my wife," Riordan said.

"Why, that's marvelous!" Mulvaney got up and slapped his desk. "Just in case anything should go wrong, he marries the other conspirator so neither can testify against the other. Ah, if I only I had a head like that, I'd have been a cardinal."

"Listen you," Mulvaney put his face close to Riordan's, "we've had enough. Lay off. Lay off Green. Keep away from the department. Far away. Why don't you and the bunco lady go somewhere it's warm as a way of getting used to where you're going to wind up. And maybe you can find a place where there aren't any Jews."

"And where would that be?"

"Oh, Taiwan. And you'd like the official way of thinking there. It starts with an absolute presumption of guilt. It shouldn't take long before they make you police commissioner."

"Now you see here," Riordan pointed a long finger at Mulvaney, "you can't talk to me like that. I am a free citizen of New York, I can do and say what I please. If you had anything on me, you'd have me in one of your sweatboxes down the hall."

Mulvaney sat down and picked up a sheet of paper. "Jeremiah, do you remember the Shomrim Society?"

"Of course I do. The Society for Cowardly Circumcised Cops, also known as the Kike Korps."

"Well, they're putting together a list, which I'm sure will be widely publicized, of particularly distinguished Jewish members of the force through the years. They were surprised, but then so delighted, to include you when I told them your mother was Jewish."

"That is a damn lie!" the old cop's face was ablaze. "I'll sue the fuckers. I'll sue them for defamation. With all the blacks on the juries in this county, I'll win a bundle."

"You might," Mulvaney said. "And then you might not. They were acting on good faith. I was acting on good faith when I told them. My father, bless his soul, told me."

"Yeah?" Riordan snarled, "But they didn't check with *me*."

"Oh they tried. At trial, records will be shown of unreturned calls, unanswered letters. But they wanted to honor you anyway."

"I'll tell them different now!"

"They will pay no attention to your modesty. It's too late."

"What the hell is this?" Riordan roared. "You're part of a criminal conspiracy. At trial, my boy, I'll be telling of this conversation."

"At trial, Jeremiah, you'll not be in my appointment book for today. Ah, the stories a feverish old man can invent and maybe even believe!"

"I'll sue the whole lot of you because I know the truth!"

"The truth?" Mulvaney leaned back. "What has that got to do with a lawsuit? You really need a rest, Jeremiah. Your mind has become confused. For example, would a clear mind want to go so deep into his pension checks to feed a lawyer to sustain a suit like this? And let us suppose that, against all odds, you win. It's a pity, Jeremiah, how long it takes for the truth, if it is the truth, to catch up with a defamation. The truth never does catch up really, not so far as most people who heard the original are concerned. Until you die, Jeremiah, you will be, to many, many people, a heroic Jewish cop. Indeed, long after you die, you'll be remembered that way and mentioned in their synagogues with reverence."

Riordan bit down hard, barely missing his tongue. "I'll be telling people _your_ mother was Jewish."

Mulvaney laughed. "Oh, you would have liked my mother. She thought they all made a living teaching young boys how to steal."

Riordan pulled on his chin. "I'm not surprised at what you've become, Mulvaney. You spend all these years using dirty tricks against your own, against working cops, why would you stop at a man who's too old and has no power to defend himself, a man who's given his life to the force?"

"Please, Jeremiah, don't go on. I forgot my handkerchief this morning."

"Fuck you!"

"That's just a bit cryptic, Jeremiah. Could it be you have a little something else to say?"

"You'll not be hearing from me," Riordan's voice was low and raspy. "You'll not be hearing from me about Green or anything else. I will never go near any precinct house. I will never report a crime to another bunch of criminals."

"You did have something else to say, I knew it, you're so shy. Your most endearing quality. Well, I'm sorry you won't be on the Shomrim honor roll." Mulvaney looked toward the door.

"Do you sleep well at night, Wilfred?" Riordan said in a soft, almost musical cadence.

"Perfectly," Mulvaney smiled.

"You will find," Riordan had moved across the room and had his hand on the doorknob, "that as the years go on, it'll take more and more booze to tuck you in safely before the light. Especially someone in your dirty line of work. I bet it's three-quarters of a fifth already before your silvery head reaches the pillow for good."

Riordan bowed. "Good-bye, dear heart, you'll see me in your dreams."

The door slammed. Mulvaney took out his keys, opened a drawer in his desk, removed a fifth of Courvoisier and a glass, poured the glass half full, and raised it. "To Jeremiah, and the pleasure of attending your wake soon, you lousy rummy." He downed the brandy, went to the door, and said cheerily, "Jeremy, would you step in?"

Jeremy came in with a sheaf of papers and photographs. "Here are the ones you wanted to see again from the soon-to-be graduates of the Police Academy. You've already marked one of them, Gardner Murray."

"Let me see him again. The face, not the background check." Mulvaney looked at the young, clear-eyed, chubby face, and put the photograph on his desk. "Yes, I want him. If he'd been born different, he could have been a nun. Lovely. Work him into my schedule tomorrow, and I'll go over the catechism with him. I'll go over these other ones later."

"He might turn you down."

"Not with those eyes he won't. A lot of practicing has gone into those eyes."

62

The tall, bony black detective walked into the Ninth Precinct and waved at the desk sergeant.

"Hey, Sam," the young, balding sergeant said, "I thought you were still on vacation."

"I'm not back to work," Sam McKibbon said. "I just have the heebie-jeebies doing nothing. You ever hear that Louis Armstrong record, Malone?"

"Can't say I have. He was before my time."

"Yes, indeed. Noah in?"

The sergeant nodded and McKibbon went upstairs.

Randall Dickerson saw him first and slapped his hand. "I thought you'd be the sheriff of Yellowstone Park by now," he said to McKibbon.

"Shit, from what I saw of those tourists, I'd rather ride shotgun for the bears. Much rather. Hello, old man," McKibbon smiled at Green who awkwardly, affectionately, patted him on the shoulder.

"What'd you do for music out there?" Green asked.

"I had my tapes, Billie and Prez and Big Ben, you know. And they played some pretty good country on the air. I think there's black in that Merle Haggard. I been reading about you boys. You come up with the rest of them corpses yet?"

"No," Fortunato Randazzo boomed from the doorway of his office. "Your partner and your stand-in think they've cleared those cases, but I don't accept incomplete corpses."

"Gotcha," McKibbon said. "But tell me," he turned to Green, "how did you tie Arthur into it?"

"His mama came in with a tape," Green said, "and on the tape was Arthur saying, 'Look Ma, it was me!' "

McKibbon filled his pipe. "I always say that with enough legwork, you can find out anything you want to know. Not that you have to do the legwork yourself."

"Why didn't you stay in Wyoming until the very end, until Sunday?" Green asked.

"You know," McKibbon lit his pipe, "I've never had an experience like that in all my life. Days, I'd walk and hike and climb and the air was so clean, so clear, I felt I'd been made clean again. By late afternoon, I'd go back to where I was staying, make myself a big vodka tonic, and just look out the window at the prairie dogs and the marmots right outside, and it was like I was a kid again and Walt Disney had arranged all of this for me.

"Yes sir, day after day, night after night, everything was as cool and tasty as a Benny Carter alto solo. I slept _good,_ better than I ever have in my life, wasn't nothing messing up my mind, and it all damn well drove me crazy.

"Yesterday I couldn't stand it anymore. One more night, and I'd have been saying to people, 'Have a good day?' and 'Isn't it a lovely morning?' and all that shit. My mind was running slower and slower, I'd clipped my toenails three times, and a librarian from Fresno, a liberal with blue hair, was telling me how much I'd like living there when I retired, which she was saying while she was tickling my knee under the table. I tell you, I never appreciated this loony bin as much as I do now. I hate to say this, where it can be used against me, but I can hardly wait until Monday morning."

"Listen," Randazzo said, "who's saying you can't catch a crook today? We got no limit. Hey, you guys, we got a new cop, fresh from the Academy, a very good kid, green as grass, I want you to meet him so he'll have somebody to go to when he can't find his elbow because it's up his ass."

Randazzo picked up the phone, and a few minutes later, a tall, chubby-faced, smiling, black, uniformed policeman came into the office. "Gardner Murray," Randazzo introduced him with a large sweep of his large hand. The new cop shook hands all around.

"Welcome to whatever this is," McKibbon said.

"Thank you, sir," the new graduate of the Police Academy said crisply. He politely declined Captain Randazzo's offer of a chair. "I'm very honored to be working here."

"Gardner," Green said, taking a cigar out of his breast pocket, "anything you want to know, anytime you need help of any kind, you come to us."

"Yes, sir!" Gardner Murray shook hands all around again. "I certainly am going to do that."

The young man left. Randazzo nodded after him. "With all due respect, gentlemen, any organization always needs young blood. Keeps all the rest of us on our toes." He reached for some hard candies in the apothecary jar on his desk. "Now, to work. That *momzer* who's been handling those whores out of the new condo off Tompkins Square Park, the one"—Randazzo glared at Green—"who's got your friend, Mendelssohn, for a lawyer, I figured out how we can bring him in. The experience should do him good. He's a very nervous little fellow. I think he's got colitis, I hope. We bust him, we soften him up for next time."

"But we don't have enough on him to bust him," Dickerson said.

"I'm not talking about the whores," Randazzo smiled. "I am talking Section 255.17 of the Penal Law. Any of you highly trained law-enforcement professionals know what that is?"

The three detectives shook their heads.

"You all look like you're on a stick," Randazzo said. "Adultery is what it is. The *momzer* is married, and he is living in that condo with a piece of poison who is not his wife."

"This is illegal?" McKibbon said. "Shit, you'd have to fill Shea Stadium with cell blocks."

"One thing at a time," Randazzo said. "In this city, I am proud to inform you, adultery is illegal. The law says: 'A person is guilty of adultery when he engages in sexual intercourse with another person at a time when he has a living spouse, or the other person has a living spouse.' God may not be in the schools, but he is in the Penal Law. Adultery is a Class B misdemeanor, and theoretically, you can get three months for that particular misdemeanor. I want that defiler of the American family brought in. Now. And cuff him tight."

"What if we see a real crime on the way?" Green got up.

The phone rang. Randazzo kept nodding, taking notes. "Funny you asked. Avenue C and Ninth Street. Man in the back of a stolen car. His eyes have been shot out. But do not forget the adulterer. Oh yeah, you might as well take the kid along, that Gardner Murray, on the homicide. He's got to start learning what to look for."